RAMAYANA

VERSUS

MAHABHARATA

My Playful Comparison

RAMAYANA
VERSUS
MAHABHARATA
A Playful Comparison

... founded by the Buddha was ... However, the king was the fountainhead of dharma; he instituted and upheld dharma. To guide him were the epics that told the story of royal families, and the conflicts they faced.

Around 1,500 ... dynasty dominated the Gangetic plains. Ram and Krishna were identified as avatars—mortal and finite forms of the immortal and infinite Vishnu on earth. With this, two separate epics—*Ramayana* and *Mahabharata*—became two chapters of a larger story, the *Vishnu Purana*. The earthly events in the epics were part of a divine drama and had cosmic implications. Ram and Krishna became ... he ... who functions differently in different spheres: one in a moral universe of Treta yuga, while the other as ... corrupt Dvapara yuga; one as king and the other as ...

This structure illustrated a fundamental principle of the Dharma-shastras: rules could change with space (desha), time (kala) and people (patra) as long as there was no violation of dharma. Dharma was thus not a set of laws; it was a way of being. It was anchored in the human ability to reverse the law of the jungle. Right from the *Shatapatha Brahmana*, dharma is linked to the moral obligation of the strong to help the weak. Adharma, on the other hand, is associated with the human submission to the animal instinct of letting the strong feed on the weak. This can only happen when we become aware of aham or the ego, born out of human insecurities. The Upanishads draw our attention to ... human insecurities. In Puranic literature, both Krishna and Vishnu's avatars... both as God, Ram and Krishna are divine as they have outgrown desires ...

RAMAYANA
VERSUS
MAHABHARATA

~ *My Playful Comparison* ~

DEVDUTT
PATTANAIK

RUPA

Published by
Rupa Publications India Pvt. Ltd 2018
7/16, Ansari Road, Daryaganj
New Delhi 110002

Sales Centres:

Allahabad Bengaluru Chennai
Hyderabad Jaipur Kathmandu
Kolkata Mumbai

ISBN: 978-93-5333-230-3

First impression 2018

10 9 8 7 6 5 4 3 2 1

Designed and typeset in Garamond by Special Effects Graphics Design Co, Mumbai
Printed by HT Media Ltd, Gr. Noida

*That which transcends measurement is
best understood by measuring, hence comparing.
Measuring is human delusion (maya),
and comparing, divine play (leela).*

*I dedicate this book to all
that can be measured and compared
as well as to that which is beyond.*

Approximate timeline of the epics, Ramayana and Mahabharata

10000 BCE:	End of ice age in subcontinent (pralaya?)
5000 BCE:	
3000 BCE:	
2500 BCE:	
1500 BCE:	Rig Veda compiled
1000 BCE:	Shatapatha Brahmana equates adharma with law of the jungle
300 BCE:	Mauryan Empire
200 BCE:	Dharma-sutras and Dharma-shastras compete for attention
100 BCE:	Indo-Greek Empire
0:	Popular oral epics are gradually put down in writing in formal Sanskrit
100 CE:	Kushan Empire
400 CE:	Cave temples with Buddhist, Jain and Hindu imagery
500 CE:	
800 CE:	Adi Shankaracharya institutionalizes Hindu monasticism
1000 CE:	Epics are formally composed in Tamil in the south
1200 CE:	Delhi Sultanate in north brings in 'Turuka dharma'
1400 CE:	Vijayanagara Empire defends Hindu dharma
1600 CE:	Epics are formally composed in Hindi in the north
1800 CE:	
1900 CE:	English translations of Sanskrit and regional epics

Contents

You will also notice how the two epics complement each other. Ram is the eldest son of a royal family while Krishna is the youngest son of a royal family. Ram upholds the rules and Krishna

Both the similarities and dissimilarities are not coincidental. This is a deliberate design to bring Vedic wisdom into the household. The work of brahmins ensures that our understanding of the world is not overshadowed by our understanding of the world. Not everyone will agree with what is being proposed in this book. That is alright too.

Introduction:
Containers of Dharma

The tradition of storytelling in India is ancient. In Vedic times, it served as entertainment between rituals. It was the responsibility of the suta, or bard, to tell tales of gods, kings and sages. Stories were of two types: Puranas and Itihasas. Puranas referred to stories of gods, kings and sages that the storyteller had simply 'heard' from others (purana = old). Itihasas, on the other hand, were stories that the storyteller had 'seen' for himself (iti = thus indeed, hasa = it happened).

The *Ramayana* and the *Mahabharata* fall in the category of Itihasa, as their composers, Valmiki and Vyasa, respectively, claimed they witnessed the events they spoke of; they even participated in the stories. This made the Itihasa far more real, and popular, than a Purana, for no one could claim they had visited the realm of the gods.

RAMAYANA tells the story of Ram, prince of Ayodhya, who on the eve of his coronation is told by his father, Dasharatha, that he should spend fourteen years in the forest in exile, and let his half-brother, Bharat, be crowned prince instead. Ram agrees to this without remorse or resentment. His wife, Sita, and brother, Lakshman, join him in the forest, where they spend their time meeting sages and fighting rakshasas. In the final year of exile, however, Sita is abducted by the rakshasa-king Ravana, because Ram rejected the advances of his sister, Surpanakha, and Lakshman mutilated her for being persistent. Ram raises an army of monkeys who build a bridge across the sea to the island kingdom of Lanka where Sita is being held captive by Ravana. Ram and the monkey army successfully rescue Sita who then undergoes a trial by fire to prove her chastity. Ram returns triumphant and is crowned king of Ayodhya, but people gossip if it is appropriate for the scion of the Raghu clan to have as his queen a woman of 'stained' reputation. So Ram abandons Sita who bears his twin sons in the forest, in the hermitage of Valmiki. The sons grow up to be mighty warriors, who learn the story of Ram from Valmiki. They also defeat Ayodhya's army, capturing Ram's royal horse, thus resisting his rule. Ram and his sons are finally reconciled. Sita bids farewell and descends into the earth; and Ram, unable to live without her, enters River Sarayu and does not rise again.

MAHABHARATA tells the story of the intense rivalry between Vyasa's grandchildren, the two branches of the Bharata clan—the five adopted sons of Pandu known as the Pandavas and the hundred sons of Dhritarashtra known as the Kauravas. Fearing that their more talented cousins would be granted the throne, the Kauravas set the Pandavas' palace on fire. The Pandavas survive and hide in the forest until they secure Draupadi, princess of Panchala, as their common wife, and Krishna of the Yadava clan, as a common friend. Empowered by a powerful wife and a wise friend, the Pandavas reveal themselves to the Bharata elders and demand their half of the family inheritance. In guilt, but with reluctance, they are given the forest of Khandava where they build the fabulous city of Indraprastha, which unfortunately, they gamble away to the Kauravas. Not content with claiming their land, the Kauravas try to disrobe Draupadi in public. Finally, it is agreed that the Pandavas will get their kingdom back after thirteen years of exile in the forest, provided they spend the final year incognito. The Pandavas agree grudgingly; Draupadi swears she will not tie her hair again until she washes it with Kaurava blood. After twelve years of wandering like pilgrims, the Pandavas enter their thirteenth and final year of exile, which they spend hiding as servants in the palace of Virata. Even after this humiliation and despite having met the conditions of their exile, the Kauravas refuse to return the Pandavas their land and war is declared. The Pandavas have seven armies and an unarmed Krishna on their side; the Kauravas have eleven armies including Krishna's army. In the battle that follows, over eighteen days, guided by Krishna, the Pandavas defeat the Kauravas, wash Draupadi's hair with the blood of the Kauravas, and reclaim their kingdom. However, the war comes at a cost—the Pandavas lose all their children. Gandhari, the mother of the Kauravas, curses Krishna that he too will witness the death of his children and grandchildren as she has, and her prophecy comes true. After a long successful reign, the Pandavas seek entry into paradise with their mortal bodies, but only Yudhishtira succeeds, only to find the Kauravas there as well! He realizes it is a struggle to share heaven with his cousins just as his cousins struggled to share the earth with the Pandavas.

The earliest references to Puranas and Itihasas can be found 2,800 years ago in the *Shatapatha Brahmana*—however, we do not know the stories that were told at the time. They may have included the story of Ram and Krishna, but we cannot be sure. A little over 2,000 years ago, after centuries of oral transmission, these stories were refined and reframed as the Sanskrit epics *Ramayana* and *Mahabharata*. It is these refined and reframed retellings that we today consider as the 'original'. It is here that the idea of dharma is elaborated for the first time in Hindu history, making them the containers of dharma for the world at large.

The word 'dharma' does not seem to be a dominant idea in Vedic times. It appears less than a hundred times in the 1,000 hymns of the *Rig Veda* that are over 3,000 years old. At the time, dharma referred to social order, as well as the royal obligation to create social order. In the *Shatapatha Brahmana*, composed sometime later, the meaning of dharma was extended to include overcoming animal instincts, reversing the law of the jungle, and creating a culture where the strong take care of the weak. In the Upanishads, dharma is barely referred to. The focus is on the atma—the wise resident of the body that witnesses the human struggle with its animal self.

The word 'dharma' gained prominence 2,300 years ago, after Emperor Ashoka used the term in his edicts. Dharma was translated into Greek as *eusebia*, which means veneration of gods, kings and parents, and in Aramaic as *qsyt*, which means truth. In other words, for the Mauryan ruler of India, dharma was both social behaviour and spiritual belief.

In the five hundred years that followed, a group of texts collectively known as the Dharma-shastras came where dharma was equated with social obligations that were based on vocation (varna dharma), stage of life (ashrama dharma), personality (sva dharma), kingship (raj dharma), womanhood (stri dharma) and monkhood (moksha dharma).

During the very same period, from the third century BCE to third century CE, the *Ramayana* and *Mahabharata*, began to receive a lot of Brahmin attention and reached their final form—the forms we are familiar with today. The stories helped people appreciate the complexities of dharma, its contextual nature (yuga dharma), subtlety (sukshma dharma), and dilemmas (dharma-sankat).

Why did dharma become such an important word after the Mauryan era, as compared to the Vedic era? Why was it important for the Brahmins to communicate this idea to the masses? Could it have something to do with Buddhism? Or maybe kingship?

Creation of the Epics

In the Vedas, celestial beings are continuously evoked for their support in living the good life. We are told that the ritual of yagna, if conducted well, results in the reward of swarga, or paradise, in the afterlife. This affirmation of worldly life and all things material waned 2,500 years ago, when the Buddha described the world as a place of suffering. He preached the cessation of desire, renouncing social life, and living as a hermit in pursuit of the oblivion of one's identity—nibbana (Pali for nirvana). He called this world view 'dhamma', which is the Pali version of the Sanskrit 'dharma'. This was radically different from the Vedic world view that connected dharma with royal obligations and social order.

Buddhist monks (Bhikkus) communicated the Buddha's ideas as Dhamma-pada—the path of dhamma. Brahmins countered this Buddhist tide by compiling and composing the Dharma-shastra, in which greater value was given to marriage, household, social obligations, and worldly life. These were two powerful and parallel discourses that evolved simultaneously and would play a key role in shaping Indian thought hereafter.

However, neither Dhamma-pada nor the Dharma-shastras appealed to the masses. The common folk preferred stories. And so, the Bhikkus composed the Jatakas, a body of literature based on popular folk tales, to teach the masses how dhamma could be practised in daily life. These tales spoke of how the Buddha practised Buddhist ideals even in his previous lives, which earned him merit and enabled him to attain nibbana in his final life. The popularity of the Jataka tales (jataka = birth conditions, astrological chart) forced the Brahmins to shift their attention from rituals and law-books to stories.

This shift had a profound effect on Hinduism—narratives such as the *Ramayana* and the *Mahabharata* took centre stage, giving rise to the story-based Puranic Hinduism, which was very different from the older, ritual-based Vedic Hinduism. This shift took place between the Mauryan and the Gupta empires, when north India was dominated by Indo-Greek (Yavana) kings, as well as the Kushanas, who came in from Central Asia.

This is also the period when both Buddhists and Brahmins began concerning themselves with the ideal of kingship. For Buddhists, the king was the protector of Buddhist dhamma.

For them, the monastic order founded by the Buddha was greater than kingship. For Brahmins, however, the king was the fountainhead of dharma; he instituted and upheld dharma. To guide him were the epics that told the story of royal families, and the conflicts they faced.

Around 1,500 years ago, when the Gupta dynasty dominated the Gangetic plains, Ram and Krishna were identified as avatars—mortal and finite forms of the immortal and infinite Vishnu on earth. With this, two separate epics—*Ramayana* and *Mahabharata*—became two chapters of a larger story, the *Vishnu Purana*. The earthly events in the epics were part of a divine drama and had cosmic implications. Ram and Krishna became two forms of the same divine being, who functions differently in different contexts, one in a more innocent Treta yuga, while the other in a more corrupt Dvapara yuga, one as king and the other as kingmaker.

This structure illustrated a fundamental principle of the Dharma-shastras: rules could change with space (desha), time (kala) and people (patra) as long as there was no violation of dharma. Dharma was thus not a set of laws; it was a way of being. It was anchored in the human ability to reverse the law of the jungle.

Right from the *Shatapatha Brahmana*, dharma is linked to the moral uprightness of the strong to help the weak. Adharma, on the other hand, is associated with the human submission to the animal instinct of letting the strong feed on the weak. This can only happen when we become aware of aham or the ego, born out of human insecurities. The Upanishads draw our attention to atma, which is free of insecurities. In Puranic literature, Ram and Krishna are visualized as embodiments of atma. Like the Buddha, Ram and Krishna are at peace as they have outgrown desires.

However, unlike the Buddha, this has not meant renunciation. Both Ram and Krishna engage with the world, as per the demands of their social contexts. They are concerned about the suffering and ignorance of those entrapped by aham around them, those who have yet to discover atma.

In other words, the two epics brought together the worldliness of the *Rig Veda*, the mystical wisdom of the Upanishads, and the directives of the Dharma-shastras. Ram in Valmiki's *Ramayana* is the embodiment of dharma. Krishna in Vyasa's *Mahabharata* enables the Pandavas to resolve ethical and moral issues known as dharma-sankat. As their stories were recounted through the ages, the word 'dharma' was repeated a thousand times. It is these epics that fired the imagination of the masses, helped them understand dharma, and made 'dharma' a common word in Hindu terminology.

Distribution and Transformation of the Epics

Plots found in the *Ramayana* and *Mahabharata* can also be found in the Jatakas, revealing a common pool of stories that informed both Brahmins and Bhikkus. But they were used differently in Buddhism, with Ram's integrity being highlighted in the *Dasharatha Jataka* and Krishna's violence being highlighted in the *Ghata Jataka*. Jains also used these stories to communicate Jain ideas and so, in Jainism, Ram is non-violent, while Krishna is violent—an attribute that delays his rise to the exalted status of Jina, one who is master of the mind.

The tension between Buddhist dhamma and Hindu dharma lasted over ten centuries. This conflict first made its way to the rest of India from the Gangetic plains, and then, across the sea to Sumatra, Java, Bali, Malaysia, Burma, Cambodia, and Thailand, as indicated by historical records and archaeological ruins there. Monks and priests travelled with merchants over mountains and seas with the stories of the Buddha, Rama and Krishna, and Indian concepts of kingship, ethics and morality.

But while Buddhist dhamma thrived in Southeast Asia, Hindu dharma prevailed in India. The reason was in all probability the social practice of caste, or jati dharma. A Brahmin was Brahmin by birth while anyone could become a Buddhist! For Hinduism to flourish across the seas, Brahmins had to travel and preach outside India. However, many orthodox Hindus saw travelling by sea as polluting, leading to loss of caste, which is why such adventures were actively discouraged. On the other hand, Buddhism encouraged the movement of monks to different lands and encouraged local people to become Buddhists. While Buddhist texts always acknowledged the role of jati in society, it had no place within the monastic order and was not essential to Buddhist dhamma.

Roughly 1,000 years ago, the Buddhist influence started waning from India. People clearly preferred the colour, drama, music, emotion, and energy associated with a householder's life. Festivals where marriages of gods were enacted captured the imagination of people and eclipsed the silence of monasteries.

Buddhism changed under Hindu influence, giving rise to

goddesses like Tara, and to the idea of Buddha-in-waiting, the Bodhisattva, who helps suffering souls with compassion, rather than simply lecturing them. This form of Buddhism spread to Central Asia and China, but in India, it was eventually eclipsed by, and absorbed into, Hinduism.

At the same time, Buddhism left its mark on Hinduism as well. Hindus, who had privileged the householder's life in the Dharmashastra, Itihasas and Puranas, now began upholding the hermit's life. Hindu monastic orders (mathas, akharas) were on the rise and they played a key role in the affairs of the temple and the state. Liberation from the world (moksha) became a key goal of life—even more important than dharma. Ram and Krishna were no longer seen as divine beings who showed humans how to live as enlightened householders but as divine beings who could help householders escape from the burdens of worldly life.

This idea of escaping from the world by submitting to a divine being was further consolidated around the twelfth century by the arrival of Islam in north India, which spoke of one God and the absolute submission to God's rules, revealed through God's messenger. Many confused the idea of avatars with the idea of prophets.

In the fourteenth century, a little over 600 years ago, the phrase 'Hindu dharma' was used for the first time, by Vijayanagara kings of the Deccan. It was used to distinguish the local way of life from 'Turuka dharma' introduced by the Central Asia warlords who had conquered much of north and south India. This is the reactionary period after which dharma gained the meaning popular today—religion.

Ideas such as moksha, bhakti, and the new definition of dharma as religion, in different measures, can be seen in the regional versions of the *Ramayana* and the *Mahabharata* that began

Approximate timeline of the epics, Ramayana and Mahabharata

10000 BCE:	End of ice age in subcontinent (pralaya?)
7000 BCE:	Traditional date ascribed to Ram
5000 BCE:	Traditional date ascribed to Krishna
3000 BCE:	Pyramids built in Egypt
2500 BCE:	Harappan Civilization
1500 BCE:	*Rig Veda*, first reference to dharma
1000 BCE:	*Shatapatha Brahmana*, equates adharma with law of the jungle
500 BCE:	The Buddha preaches dhamma
300 BCE:	Mauryan Empire
200 BCE:	Dhamma-pada and Dharma-shastras compete for attentior.
100 BCE:	Indo-Greek Empire
0:	Popular oral epics are gradually put down in writing in formal Sanskrit
100 CE:	Kushan Empire
200 CE:	*Artha-shastra, Kama-shastra, Natya-shastra*
300 CE:	Gupta Empire
400 CE:	Cave temples with Buddhist, Jain and Hindu imagery
500 CE:	Construction of free-standing stone temples begins
800 CE:	Adi Shankaracharya institutionalizes Hindu monasticism
1000 CE:	Epics are formally composed in Tamil in the south
1200 CE:	Delhi Sultanate in north brings in 'Turuka dharma'
1400 CE:	Vijayanagara Empire defends 'Hindu dharma'
1600 CE:	Epics are formally composed in Hindi in the north
1800 CE:	British Raj
1900 CE:	English translations of Sanskrit and regional epics

appearing with greater frequency in the centuries that followed. In Tamil, Telugu, Assamese, Odia, Bengali, Kannada, Malayalam, Maithili, Awadhi, Marathi, Gujarati, and Marwari, poets began composing passionate songs beseeching Ram and Krishna to save them from a world that was cruel and unjust. Emotion (bhakti) was valued over action (karma) and intellect (gyan). The Bhakti movement peaked across India 500 years ago. Such was its popularity that even the Mughal King Akbar had the *Ramayana* and the *Mahabharata* translated in Persian and lavishly illustrated by court painters.

After the British conquered India about 200 years ago, they started the work of translating and analysing the *Ramayana* and the *Mahabharata*. These were retold using the linear European template of heroes (Ram, Krishna), villains (Ravana, Kauravas) and victims (Sita, Pandavas). Many wondered if like Greek myths, these epics were proto-history, or just fantasy.

Making sense of the epics

This colonial influence lingers even today. Left-leaning Hindus have reduced the *Ramayana* and *Mahabharata* to epics that promote 'Brahminical hegemony' based on patriarchy and casteism, while Right-leaning Hindus insist Ram and Krishna were noble and egalitarian historical figures who lived 7,000 and 5,000 years ago, respectively, absence of archaeological data notwithstanding. They blame 'a thousand years of slavery' for the loss of Hindu memory. Today, the role played by the two epics in transmitting the Hindu concept of dharma has been nearly forgotten. Savage political battles are being fought to transform the two great epics of India from 'records of timeless wisdom' to 'records of the past'.

If you prefer to see the two epics as containers of timeless Vedic wisdom, as they were meant to be, you will notice that both stories have:

- *Identical building blocks*: childless kings, disputed kingship, ambitious queens, deer hunts, quarrelling brothers, forest exile, war, violation of women, killing of Brahmins, and authors who also participate in the story they are recounting.

- *Identical structure*: disputes over inheritance leading to forest exile, where dystopia is experienced; forming of allies before a war is fought, won, and before tragedy finally strikes.

- *Identical theme*: struggle to rise above the animal within and the forest without, in different social contexts.

The identical structure of the two epics

Ramayana Chapters (kanda)	Mahabharata Chapters (parva)	Theme
1	1	The long prologue where the author explains how he came to write the story, how he is part of the story, and the dynastic history of the protagonists, which is why the epic is an Itihasa, not a Purana.
2	2	Palace intrigue results in Dasharatha asking Ram to go to the forest, and the Pandavas, too, go to the forest after gambling away their kingdom in a game of dice fixed by the Kauravas.
3	3	The years spent in the forest wandering, hunting deer, fighting demons, visiting sages and holy spots by both Ram and the Pandavas.
4	4	Experience of alternate realities as Ram encounters the kingdom of monkeys where brothers fight over a kingdom, while the Pandavas live secret lives as servants of a king whose brother-in-law abuses power.
5	5	Preparations for war as Hanuman travels over the sea to give Ram's message to Ravana and Krishna tries in vain to broker peace with the Kauravas.
6	6-11	War and bloodshed, which leads to the death of family members.
7	12-18	Aftermath of the war, with Ram banishing his wife and facing his own mortality with grace, and the Pandavas having to cope with the death of their parents, Krishna, and their own mortality.

You will also notice how the two epics complement each other. Ram is the eldest son of a royal family while Krishna is the youngest son of a cowherd family. Ram is unaware of his divinity; Krishna is fully aware of his divinity. Ram is a rule-follower; Krishna is a rule-bender. Ram is king; Krishna is kingmaker.

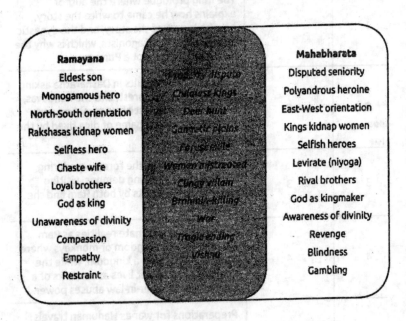

Ramayana		Mahabharata
Eldest son	*Property dispute*	Disputed seniority
Monogamous hero	*Childless kings*	Polyandrous heroine
North-South orientation	*Deer hunt*	East-West orientation
Rakshasas kidnap women	*Gambling picnic*	Kings kidnap women
Selfless hero	*Forest exile*	Selfish heroes
Chaste wife	*Women mistreated*	Levirate (niyoga)
Loyal brothers	*Cunning villain*	Rival brothers
God as king	*Brahmin-killing*	God as kingmaker
Unawareness of divinity	*War*	Awareness of divinity
Compassion	*Tragic ending*	Revenge
Empathy	*Vishnu*	Blindness
Restraint		Gambling

These similarities and dissimilarities are neither accidental nor coincidental. This is a deliberate design to bring Vedic wisdom into the household. The work of Brahmins eager to ensure Vedic understanding of the world is not overshadowed by the Buddhist understanding of the world. Not everyone will agree with what is being proposed in this book. That is alright, for:

Within infinite myths, lies an eternal truth
Who sees it all?
Varuna has but a thousand eyes
Indra, a hundred
You and I, only two

I

Narration

In which we explore how the two epics emerged in the same context, had very similar creators and audiences, and how they incorporated Vedic and Puranic elements over time.

1

Both are products of the same geography and history

Ram travelled from the Gangetic plains to the southern coast 7,000 years ago, while Krishna migrated from the Gangetic plains to the western coast 5,000 years ago. This is traditional lore, based on astrological information. However, this is not based on what historians consider evidence.

At the Maharaja Sayajirao University Oriental Institute of Baroda, various versions of the oldest *Ramayana* have been collected from different parts of India. Scholars used this archive to put together a critical edition of the *Ramayana*, compiling verses they felt to be the oldest and most authentic. In this version, there is no mention of 'Lakshman Rekha'; Ravana simply picks Sita up in the absence of Ram and Lakshman. Likewise, at the Bhandarkar Oriental Research Institute, Pune, a critical edition from the oldest extant versions of the *Mahabharata* was put together by scholars. In this version, Krishna does not come to Draupadi's rescue in the gambling hall; bad omens force the Kauravas to stop. Of course, scholars disagree on which verses constitute the earliest versions and which do not.

Broadly, a linguistic analysis of these texts reveals that they follow grammar rules which are absent in the early Vedic texts. These grammar rules were collated by Pāṇini 2,500 years ago. The Vedas are pre-Pāṇini while the two epics are post-Pāṇini.

The earliest portions of these epics are 2,300 years old, while the most recent portions are 1,700 years old. This means the texts were put down in writing between the Mauryan and the Gupta periods, when much of north India was ruled by Indo-Greek (Yavana) and Kushana kings, while the Deccan was controlled by the Satavahana kings.

Scholars have also found clues in the many layers of storytelling in these two narratives. For example, the language used in the first and last chapters of the *Valmiki Ramayana* is very different from that of the five chapters in the middle. Stories and dialogues were clearly composed and recomposed by many scholars, who transmitted these to students and family members over generations, leading to many variations. Initially, the transmission was oral. Writing came much later. We know that writing became widespread in India only after Ashoka's reign—around 2,300 years ago. Therefore, stories of Ganesha writing the *Mahabharata* for Vyasa, or Hanuman writing Ram's name on rocks thrown into the sea came into existence much later.

The stories of Ram and Krishna were most probably based on, or inspired by, events that took place before 1000 CE, i.e. over 3,000 years ago, in the Gangetic plains. This is where pottery dating to the Vedic period has been found, at places traditionally associated with the two epics.

Buddhists and Jains, who started distancing themselves from the Brahmins 2,500 years ago, were also aware of these stories. The three groups transmitted these tales orally long before writing them down. This common origin explains why we find plots similar to the *Ramayana* and *Mahabharata* in the Buddhist Jatakas and Jain Agamas.

Brahmins, Buddhists and Jains travelled from the Gangetic plains to the south. The earliest Tamil 'Sangam' literature shows familiarity with the two epics and speaks of kings who fed the armies at Kurukshetra. This reveals that the *Ramayana* and *Mahabharata* had reached the southernmost tip of India at least 2,000 years ago, if not earlier.

Which of the two epics came first? We know Vedic culture covered the expanse from Punjab to the Gangetic plains because the *Rig Veda* refers more to Sindhu (Indus) and the now-dry Saraswati than to Ganga, while the *Shatapatha Brahmana* refers to the journey across Gomti, which separates the Upper Gangetic plain from the Lower Gangetic plain. The story of the *Mahabharata* is restricted to the Upper Gangetic plains, to the regions known as Kuru-Panchala, whereas the *Ramayana* reveals familiarity with Lower Gangetic plains of Videha, and then proceeds to the world beyond the Vindhyas and Kishkinda. Additionally, the *Ramayana* reveals a more refined family structure as compared to the *Mahabharata*. This has led scholars to believe that the events of the *Mahabharata* probably took place earlier.

Others have argued that Krishna's story extends the narrative to include the Lower Gangetic plains of Magadha and stretches further east to Assam, as well as the western coast of India, in Dwarka. The *Jain Mahabharata* turns the story into a conflict between Krishna of Dwarka and Jarasandha of Magadha, shifting the geography to the Lower Gangetic plains. Hence, according to this version, the events of the *Mahabharata* must have occurred later. Those with this view also point to the fact that within the *Mahabharata*, the story of the *Ramayana* is presented to the Pandavas by the rishis as history, whereas in the *Ramayana*, Ram has no knowledge of the Pandavas.

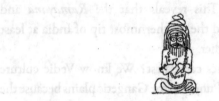

2

Both are composed by witnesses, who are rishis

Although many writers contributed to the Sanskrit and regional 'texts', the original *Ramayana* is attributed to Valmiki and the original *Mahabharata* is attributed to Vyasa. Both these rishis or poet-sages claimed to have witnessed the events that they wrote about, which is why the two epics are assertively called Itihasa— 'thus indeed it happened'.

But first, who were the rishis?

Hindus believe that long ago a group of men and women became sensitive to certain vibrations in the cosmos. They began to hear what others could not hear, and see what others could not see. These were the rishis, or seers. They composed hymns (mantras) from what they heard and saw, these mantras together formed verses (rig), which they bound together to create poems (sukta), which were then bunched into chapters (mandalas). This collection (samhita) of verses came to be known as the *Rig Veda*, as it was clear that the hymns contained the wisdom (vidya) of the gods. The language of composition came to be known as Sanskrit—the perfectly formed language of the gods. Hymns of the *Rig Veda* were put to music in the *Sama Veda*. They were attached to rituals in the *Yajur Veda*. A few turned into spells in the *Atharva Veda*. These rituals were explained in manuals known as Brahmanas. The ideas underlying the hymns were explored in the Aranyakas and discussed in the Upanishads. They revealed 'brahman'—the architecture of the human mind, its unique ability to outgrow hunger and fear, expand the mind, and eventually realize infinity.

This was Vedic wisdom. It was contained in the Samhitas, Brahmanas, Aranyakas and Upanishads. Those who memorized and communicated these containers of 'brahman' over generations were called Brahmins. If rishis were the *transponders* who received Vedic wisdom from the cosmos, Brahmins were the *transmitters* who took the containers of that wisdom—not the wisdom itself—to the people.

Both Valmiki and Vyasa were rishis, not Brahmins, transponders, not transmitters of wisdom. Valmiki descended from Bhrigu rishi. Vyasa was the son of Parasara, the grandson of Vasishtha. Bhrigu and Vasishtha were two of the seven primaeval sages (sapta-rishis) who were Brahma's mind-born sons (manas-putras).

Valmiki's name refers to the termite hill that arose around him as he meditated in perfect stillness for a thousand years. Vyasa's name means the organizer, for he gathered scattered Vedic hymns and put them together systematically.

As noted earlier, both Valmiki and Vyasa witnessed and participated in the events they described in the epics. Valmiki gave shelter to Sita after Ram cast her out of Ayodhya, following malicious gossip; he helped her raise her two children; taught them the *Ramayana*; and even testified to the purity of Sita before Ram. Vyasa made the widowed queens of Vichitravirya pregnant, which makes him the biological father of Dhritarashtra by Ambika, and of Pandu by Ambalika, and therefore, the grandfather of the Kauravas and Pandavas.

Both Valmiki and Vyasa were driven to compose their works in anguish. Valmiki saw a hunter shoot down a male bird, and heard the wailing of its mate. Enraged, he cursed the hunter. The curse came out in the form of poetry. He decided to compose the story of Ram as poetry, where Sita wails for Ram, Mandodari for Ravana, and Tara for Vali. This made him the 'first poet' (adi kavi) in the world. Vyasa helplessly witnessed his grandchildren killing each other over property on the battlefield of Kurukshetra. Raising his arms, he wondered aloud why people did not follow dharma, even though it guaranteed artha and kama in this life, and moksha in the next.

3

Both are narrated before kings, who have a stake in the story

In Vedic times, the yajaman was the patron and beneficiary of a yagna (ritual). The yagna was conducted by Brahmins, during which they invited gods to partake of offerings and grant their grace and blessings to the yajaman. Storytelling was the most popular mode of entertainment during these rituals, which sometimes stretched for months, even years. In both the *Ramayana* and the *Mahabharata*, the yajaman is always the king (raja), hence a Kshatriya (one who oversees a territory or kshetra). The *Ramayana* is narrated during Ram's yagna and the *Mahabharata*, during Janamejaya's yagna.

Ram's yagna is the ashwamedha yagna that establishes his rule over the region traversed by the royal horse. He hears the epic, the narration of his own story, from the mouths of two young students of the poet-sage Valmiki—Luv and Kush—who are his own sons; only he does not know it. This creates a dramatic setting—a king listening to his own tale from the mouths of two youths, who are in fact his own sons. The tale describes Ram's greatness and yet the two narrators are victims of Ram's rigid adherence to not-so-great family rules that demanded he abandon their mother—his wife—to protect family rituals. Thus, we are made to think about how a hero in one context is a villain in another.

A similar dramatic setting marks the first narration of the *Mahabharata*. Janamejaya is conducting a yagna to kill all the snakes in the world as revenge against a snake called Takshaka who killed his father, Parikshit. During this yagna, Vyasa's student Vaisampayana narrates the story of Janamejaya's ancestors, and during its narration we realize how Janamejaya's ancestors, the Bharatas, earned the ire of the serpent people (naga) by burning their forest. Thus, we appreciate the role of karma in our lives. We think we are victims, when in fact, in a larger narrative, we turn out to be villains.

Vaisampayana's narration is heard by Romaharshana, a bard, who narrates it to his son, Ugrashrava, who then narrates it to the sage Shaunaka, and his followers, in the Naimisha forest—the same forest where Ram had heard the *Ramayana* for the first time from the mouths of Luv and Kush. In the Puranic tradition, the storyteller (suta) becomes more important than the ritual priest (Brahmin). What was expressed through ritual, chanting and mime in Vedic times, is expressed later through character and plot.

What is interesting is that neither in the *Ramayana* nor in the *Mahabharata* do we actually hear the story from the mouth of the composer. We hear it via the students. In both the epics, it is first narrated to the very people whose story is being told—Valmiki tells the story of Ram to Ram through Luv and Kush; Vyasa tells the story of the Bharata kings to a Bharata king through Vaisampayana.

4

Both have Vedic gods as subordinate characters

Yagna, the primary ritual of the Vedic period, is referred to in the very first hymn of the *Rig Veda*. The gods who were invoked during the yagna were mainly Indra (god of victory), Agni (fire-messenger), Soma (sap of a plant), and to a lesser degree, Varuna (god of morality), Surya (sun-god), Vayu (wind-god), the Ashwini twins (solar gods) and Yama (god of death). Both the *Ramayana* and *Mahabharata* refer to the yagna ritual and a few Vedic gods, but they clearly play subsidiary and supporting roles.

In the *Ramayana*, the yagna enables the birth of Ram. A Vedic ritual involving the ploughing of the earth gives Janaka a daughter, Sita. Hanuman, Sugriva and Vali are said to be the children of Vayu, Surya and Indra, respectively, by vanara women. In the *Mahabharata*, by the power of mantras, Kunti invokes Surya, Yama (also called Dharma), Vayu and Indra, and bears Karna, Yudhishthira, Bhima and Arjuna. Madri invokes the celestial Ashwini twins, and is blessed with Nakula and Sahadeva. Drupada, too, creates the twins, Draupadi and Dhrishtadyumna, through the yagna.

Agni plays a key role in both epics. In the *Ramayana*, he is part of the Agni-pariksha, or fire-trial. Sita walks into fire to prove she is chaste, and Agni emerges and tells Ram to accept her because not only is she pure but also because he is Vishnu, and should not be bound by human pettiness in matters of fidelity. In regional variations, the real Sita hides in the realm of Agni while Ravana takes a duplicate Sita to Lanka. Thus, fire protects Sita's purity. In the *Mahabharata*, Agni regains his lustre when he consumes the forest of Khandava and clears it, allowing the Pandavas to build the city of Indraprastha. Thus, burning the forest is not seen as wanton destruction born out of ambition, but an act of feeding a Vedic god weakened by hunger. This indicates the waning influence of the Vedic gods by the time the two epics reached their mature form.

In the *Ramayana*, Indra seduces Gautama's wife Ahalya and is cursed by Gautama. There is also the story of Ram blinding Indra's son Jayanta in one eye when he harasses Sita in the form of a crow. Ravana's son Meghanad defeats Indra and so, he is known as Indrajit. Indra also provides Ram with a celestial chariot in his fight against Ravana. In the *Mahabharata*, the Pandavas seek entry into Indra's swarga, where all hungers are indulged. But during the course of the story they are informed that there is a higher heaven—that of Vishnu—where there is freedom from rebirth. This indicates the shift from the older Vedic Hinduism to later Puranic Hinduism.

5

Both are trials of Vishnu, the preserver

In Puranic Hinduism, the abstract ideas of the Vedas—expressed ritually and poetically—are transformed into stories replete with plots and characters that common people can understand. Here, for the first time, we encounter the idea of the Hindu trinity—Brahma, Vishnu and Shiva. Brahma is visualized as a Brahmin, Vishnu as a king and Shiva as an ascetic.

Despite the high status given to Brahmins in Hindu society, the priest-like Brahma is not worshipped. He and his sons—the devas and the asuras, the rakshasas and the yakshas, the birds and the serpents—are seen as creatures who are hungry and insecure, and therefore, unworthy of adoration.

By contrast, Vishnu and Shiva are seen as having outgrown their hunger and insecurity, and are therefore, worthy of adoration. The difference between Shiva and Vishnu is that Shiva needs to be coaxed to participate in society and engage with Brahma's children, whereas Vishnu does so willingly. The *Ramayana* and the *Mahabharata* are essentially stories of how Vishnu engages with society. He is immortal and infinite, but in the two epics, he takes mortal and finite forms—the avatars!

Vishnu takes the form of Ram and Krishna for various reasons. In some stories, he does this to liberate his doorkeepers, Jaya and Vijaya, who were cursed to be born on earth (as Ravana and Shishupala) by sages whose entry into Vishnu's abode they obstructed during the call of duty. In other stories, however, this descent is to relieve the burden of Bhoo-devi, the earth-goddess, who is tired of the greed of kings who are supposed to take care of her. In these stories, Vishnu is forced by Brahmins to go to earth and restore dharma; and so, in many images, Vishnu sports the footprint of Bhrigu, the archetypical complaining Brahmin, on his right shoulder.

Our understanding of the shift from Vedic to Puranic Hinduism is based on hindsight. Naturally, this shift, which took place over centuries, was not obvious to those experiencing it. To get a sense of the haphazard way in which this great change took place, we have to study the chronology of the texts documenting the stories we are now so familiar with.

The *Ramayana* and the *Mahabharata* are the first story-collections we have. They may be seen as 2,000-year-old proto-Puranas where the link between Ram and Krishna to Vishnu is not very obvious. The earliest Purana dedicated to Vishnu in which the word 'avatar' first appears is 1,500 years old. The Purana dedicated to Shiva came around the same time, but the one dedicated to the goddess (devi), embodied as the sovereign Durga or Chandi, came approximately 1,300 years ago.

Arguably the most sophisticated Purana, the *Bhagavata Purana*, reached its most refined form about 1,000 years ago, and in it, we find another shift—the rise of bhakti, the emotional connection that binds the devotee to their chosen deity. So, the ritual nature of Hinduism, which was dominant 3,000 years ago, gave way to the narrative form 2,000 years ago, which in turn, took an emotional form about 1,000 years ago. It was a journey from karma to gyan to bhakti. We find the three aspects in every age, but the proportion varies.

Today, the *Ramayana* and *Mahabharata* are seen as elaborations of the *Vishnu Purana*. They reveal to us how a prince and a cowherd used Vedic wisdom to live worldly lives, negotiating with hungry and insecure relatives and strangers. Ram and Krishna are both responsible householders and detached hermits at the same time. More importantly, chanting the name of Ram and Krishna solves worldly problems and liberates us from earthly bondage.

6

Both involve the rescue of the goddess, who embodies the world

While there are goddesses who are early forms of Lakshmi and Saraswati—such as Shri and Vak—in the Vedas, the worship of the warrior goddesses, Durga and Kali, came into prominence much later. Kotravai, a goddess mentioned in the 2,000-year-old Tamil Sangam literature is perhaps the first reference of a goddess who loves war and consumes blood. The first image of Durga is found in the Ellora caves and Pallava temples, dating back to the seventh century CE. Not surprisingly, it is only in later layers, and in Tantrik and folk retellings of the *Ramayana* and *Mahabharata*, that the role of the goddess is elaborated.

The Goddess is visualized in two forms: as the mother—one who can take care of herself and hence the world, and as the daughter—one who needs protection. As mother, she is nature, wild and untamed; Kali or Chandi. As daughter, she is culture, the demure and auspicious; Gauri or Vimala or Mangala, one who embodies wealth (Lakshmi), power (Durga) and knowledge (Saraswati). She shuns Brahma, turns Shiva from a hermit to a householder, and seeks Vishnu's protection.

Before war, both Ram and the Pandavas evoke Durga, the goddess of war, and patron of kings. It is said that Durga was traditionally worshipped in spring (vasanta) for nine nights; Ram shifted the worship to autumn (sharad) so he could obtain the blessings of the Goddess before going to war. Five hundred years ago, the medieval Bengali poet Krittibas translated the *Ramayana* in Bengali, narrating the story of Ram offering his eye to Durga to make up for the shortage of a single lotus flower that he wishes to offer the Goddess. Impressed by his devotion, the Goddess appears before him and blesses him. In Tamil retellings of the *Mahabharata*, the Pandavas discover late one night that their wife is no ordinary woman but a goddess who hunts elephants and buffaloes at night to quench her thirst until the great war, when her husbands will kill her abusers, the Kauravas, and satisfy her completely. They realize that if they do not accomplish this, she will herself kill the Kauravas, and then proceed to consume the entire world that does not care to protect her.

In the Sanskrit *Adbhut Ramayana*, composed 500 years ago, Sita takes the form of Durga to kill the thousand-headed son of Ravana whom Ram is unable to defeat. Similarly, in the

Bengali *Mahabharata, Bharat Panchali*—composed by Kavi Sanjay around the same period—we learn how after Abhimanyu's death, when the Pandavas refuse to fight their guru, Drona, who commands the Kaurava forces at night, Draupadi and her daughters-in-law, along with the other women of the Pandava camp, take the Pandavas's weapons and defeat the Kauravas.

In her temples, the Goddess is often seen in the company of two male deities—Hanuman and Bhairava. In the *Ramayana*, Hanuman serves the Goddess, helping Ram rescue her by sacrificing the sorcerer Mahiravana to Kali (in the *Adbhuta Ramayana*). But he stays celibate and never looks upon her with eyes of desire, which is why he becomes her eternal guardian. In the *Mahabharata*, Bhima is often linked to Bhairava, for just as Bhairava beheads those who look upon the Goddess with lust, Bhima kills everyone—from the Kichaka to Kauravas—who abuse Draupadi (the embodiment of the Goddess). Like Bhairava, Bhima drinks the blood of the Kauravas and washes Draupadi's unbound hair with it.

7

Both include devotees of Shiva, the destroyer

In the *Ramayana*, Ravana is described as Shiva's most ardent devotee. Ravana composes the 'Rudra-stotra', a song in praise of Shiva, and designs the Rudra-vina, a lute dedicated to Shiva; using his heads as the gourd, his hands as the beams and his nerves as the strings. He even seeks to carry Mount Kailash to his home in Lanka, but is stopped by Shiva who presses his big toe against the mountain slope and creates so much pressure that Ravana buckles and gets trapped under the mountain, begging for forgiveness. He then obtains from Shiva a special sword known as Chandrahasa. After killing Ravana, Ram establishes a Shiva-linga at Rameswaram, to thank Shiva for his help and to apologize for killing his devotee.

In the *Mahabharata*, Arjuna gets the Pashupata missile from Shiva. And just as Shiva crushes Ravana's pride, Shiva also humbles Arjuna. During the exile, Arjuna goes to the forest and prays to Shiva when a wild boar disturbs him. Irritated, he shoots the wild boar. Later, he is surprised to find the boar struck with two arrows, not one. A tribal hunter or Kirata claims that he has shot the animal. The entitled prince dismisses the hunter's claim and is challenged to a duel to prove his worthiness. In the fight that follows, Arjuna realizes that the tribal is more than a match for him. Defeated and humbled, he recognizes Shiva in the hunter and begs for forgiveness. He is thus granted the Pashupata missile.

Shiva is the god who takes no sides—in the *Ramayana*, he supports both Ram and Ravana; in the *Mahabharata*, he supports both the Pandavas and Kauravas. Shiva gives the Pashupata to Arjuna, and he blesses Drupada with the children, Shikhandi, Dhrishtadyumna and Draupadi, who eventually become the cause of the death of the Kauravas, Drona and Bhishma. Shiva also helps Ashwathama kill Drupada, Shikhandi, Dhrishtadyumna, and all of Draupadi's children in their sleep, on the night following the end of the Kurukshetra war.

Many see the *Ramayana* and *Mahabharata* as revealing the rivalry between Shiva worshippers (Shaivas) and Vishnu worshippers (Vaishnavas). So Ram, who is Vishnu's avatar, kills Ravana, who is Shiva's devotee. And in the *Mahabharata*, Krishna, who is Vishnu's avatar, kills various worshippers of Shiva, including Bana, king of Sonitapura; Kalyavana, who attacked Mathura on Jarasandha's orders; Kashiraja, who attacked Dwarka to avenge the death of his friend, the king of Paundarka; and Shalva, who attacked Dwarka with his flying chariot.

Others see the *Ramayana* and *Mahabharata* as uniting Shiva and Vishnu. So when Vishnu descends as Ram, Shiva comes as his younger brother, Lakshman, who is quick-tempered and lacks Ram's patience. When Vishnu becomes Krishna, Shiva becomes his elder brother, Balarama, also short-tempered and unable to understand Krishna's guile. In Hindu iconography, Lakshman and Balarama are shown as white-complexioned, like Shiva, while Ram and Krishna are depicted as black or blue, like Vishnu. In the Bhakti period, many began to see the celibate and detached Hanuman as an avatar of Shiva, who helps Ram, and inspires Arjuna.

In both epics, there is mention of Ram and the Pandavas establishing Shiva temples during their respective years in forest exile. Ram prays to Shiva in Rameswaram in the south and Rishikesh in the north to cleanse himself of the sin of killing a Brahmin, Ravana, and the many rakshasas of Lanka. In Kedarnath, the story goes that after killing the Kauravas, the Pandavas went to the Himalayas to cleanse themselves of the demerit earned from killing their cousins, the Kauravas, their brother, Karna, their teacher, Drona and their foster father, Bhishma. Shiva refused to meet them and ran away, taking the form of a bull. But the Pandavas tried to catch hold of him forcibly, tearing the bull apart, each piece becoming a Shiva-linga that is worshipped in the Himalayan region. In Puri, Odisha, it is said that the Pandavas visited Jagannath during the year when they were in disguise, and each one of them established a temple dedicated to Shiva in the vicinity. Similar stories of Ram and/or the Pandavas establishing Shiva temples can also be found in Maharashtra and Kerala.

II

Family

In which we discuss how our two epics are family dramas anchored by childless fathers, ambitious mothers, supportive siblings and spouses.

8

Both are family disputes
over property

To appreciate the similarity between the *Ramayana* and the *Mahabharata*, we have to contrast them with the two great Greek epics, *The Iliad* and *The Odyssey*. Both Greek epics are based on the Greek siege of Troy, which lasted over ten years, to bring back Helen, the Greek queen who had eloped with a Trojan prince named Paris. *The Iliad* tells the story of the Greek hero Achilles in the final year of the war, while the *The Odyssey* tells the story of Odysseus's long journey home.

Achilles is furious when he is asked to give up his concubine to the leader of the Greek army and so he withdraws from the battlefield. The result is disastrous. The Greek army faces numerous defeats. Achilles returns to battle only to savagely avenge the death of his lover, Patroclus. This return marks the beginning of the fall of Troy, also called Ilium—hence the title, *The Iliad*. When Troy finally falls and has been brutally plundered, the Greeks return home. Odysseus, however, faces numerous obstacles on the way owing to the wrath of the sea-god, Poseidon. These include encounters with monsters such as Scylla and Charybdis, and nymphs like the Sirens, Calypso and Circe. He reaches Ithaca ten years after he leaves Troy, twenty years after leaving home, and is pleased to find his wife, Penelope, faithfully waiting for him.

Both stories deal with individuals and their struggles with power and authority. They mirror the Western obsession with individualism and heroism, and the battle against villainy and oppression—a theme carried forward by biblical prophets and comic-book superheroes. While the Greek hero fights for himself, biblical prophets fight for the tribe, and the superhero fights to save a city or the world.

By contrast, the *Ramayana* and the *Mahabharata* are essentially family dramas, where individuals exist in an ecosystem of co-dependence with others, like a tree in a forest. There is neither the isolationist individualism of the Greek epics nor the overpowering demand for the tribal allegiance of biblical narratives. The Indian epics are all about relationships.

The *Ramayana* deals with the solar dynasty, and the *Mahabharata* with the lunar dynasty. These are the two arms to which most Hindu kings traced their lineage in order to establish the legitimacy of their rule. In both epics, we encounter different families and their politics.

In the *Ramayana*, we encounter the family tensions in the vanara kula of Kishkinda and in the rakshasa kula of Lanka. In the *Mahabharata*, there is mention of the Yadu kula whose daughter is married to the Pandava branch of the Kuru clan, and the Gandhara kula whose daughter is married into the Kaurava branch. In both epics, crisis follows family quarrels over inheritance. He who keeps the family united is good; he who divides the family is bad. The families in both epics deal with Kshatriyas and the dispute is often between brothers over inheritance.

In the *Ramayana*, the tension involves three sets of brothers:

- Ram and Bharat in Ayodhya—Bharat refuses to take advantage of his mother's opportunism and insists that Ram, the elder son, will always be the king.

- Sugriva and Vali in Kishkinda—although asked to share the kingdom by their father, the stronger brother, Bali, drives Sugriva, the weaker one, out following a misunderstanding.

- Kubera and Ravana in Lanka—Kubera is driven out of the city he built by his younger and stronger brother, Ravana, who declares himself the king.

In the *Mahabharata*, too, similar tensions exist around who is the rightful king of Hastinapur. Legitimacy becomes increasingly complicated with each passing generation, revealing the fragility of rules associated with inheritance.

- Bhishma abdicates to make room for his weaker half-brothers—Chitrasena, who dies young, and Vichitravirya, who is too weak to find himself a wife.

- Vichitravirya's younger son, Pandu, is made king because the elder son, Dhritarashtra, is born blind. But while Pandu cannot father children on his own, Dhritarashtra is so virile that he fathers a hundred sons.

- Yudhishthira, eldest of the five foster sons of Pandu, is born before Duryodhana, eldest of the hundred sons of Dhritarashtra, even though the latter is conceived first.

This theme of brothers fighting over property can be traced to the gods themselves, indicating its eternal nature. From Brahma, the first living being (jiva), emerges his mind-born son, Kashyapa, whose many wives give birth to many children who are constantly fighting amongst themselves.

- Diti's children, the daityas, fight Aditi's sons, the adityas, which eventually becomes the battle of the asuras and devas over paradise (swarga).

- Kadru's children, the nagas, fight Vinata's son, Garuda, over nectar (amrita).

- Pulatsya's descendants, the children of Vishravana, the yakshas and the rakshasas, born of two different mothers, keep fighting for supremacy of the forests, and finally for peace; the yakshas move north to be ruled by Kubera and the rakashas move south to be ruled by Ravana.

The fact that all living creatures descend from Brahma makes all living creatures siblings. Hence the maxim: vasudhaiva kutumbakam, the whole world is family. However, this is not a happy family. This is a family that keeps fighting over resources, over territory, over property.

9

Both begin with childless kings

The plot of the *Ramayana* and the *Mahabharata* starts with stories of childless kings, who need divine intervention to father sons.

In the *Ramayana*, Dasharatha, the king of Ayodhya, has three wives but no children. And so, he invites Rishyashringa to conduct a yagna that will enable him to bear sons. Rishyashringa, we are told, has magical powers that are linked to his celibacy and lack of awareness of women. His father, a celibate sage called Vibhandaka, lost control over his senses at the sight of a beautiful woman and expelled semen, which was ingested by a female deer. The doe gave birth to Rishyashringa, who had horns like his mother. He grew up without the knowledge of women and so a courtesan was sent to enchant him and bring him to Dasharatha's palace. In a few regional and folk *Ramayanas*, the woman sent to fetch Rishyashringa is not a courtesan but Dasharatha's daughter, Shanta, who had been given away in adoption to Lomasha. Rishyashringa is able to bring rain to the drought-ridden kingdom of Lomasha and so it is expected that with his ascetic powers he will be able to bring children to the childless royal household of Ayodhya. He succeeds in pleasing the gods, and from the ritual fire appears a celestial being who gives Dasharatha a pot of elixir that promises to give sons to the woman who drinks it. Dasharatha divides the elixir equally between his senior queen, Kaushalya, and his favourite queen, Kaikeyi, both of whom give half their share to the youngest queen, Sumitra. And so, the three queens bear Dasharatha four sons—Kaushalya bears Ram, Kaikeyi bears Bharat, and Sumitra bears the twins, Lakshman and Shatrughna.

In the *Mahabharata*, Bhishma takes a vow of celibacy to assure his stepmother, Satyavati, that he will have no son who would challenge the rights of his half-brothers, born of Satyavati, to the throne of Hastinapur. Only then does Satyavati marry Shantanu, king of Hastintapur. But Satyavati bears two weakling sons. One dies at an early age following a duel. The other son, Vichitravirya, is unable to find himself a wife. So Bhishma abducts three princesses of Kashi, and gets two of them—Ambika and Ambalika—to marry Vichitravirya. Vichitravirya dies before fathering a child. Satyavati summons Vyasa, her son by Parasara, born before her marriage to Shantanu, and asks him to accept the widows. Like Rishyashringa, he too is a celibate ascetic. But instead of a yagna invoking a magic potion from the gods, Vyasa is being asked to go to the queens himself. Vyasa requests time to make himself presentable. An impatient Satyavati refuses to give him time and so, unprepared, he goes to the chambers of the two queens, who end up bearing deformed children—a blind Dhritarashtra and a pale, probably impotent, Pandu. Pandu is able to father children only after his wives chant a mantra and invoke the gods. Yama, Vayu and Indra give Kunti three sons—Yudhishthira, Bhima and Arjuna. The Ashwini twins give Madri twin sons—Nakula and Sahadeva.

In the *Ramayana*, the yagna conducted by a virile hermit helps Dasharatha father four sons with the intervention of the gods.

In the *Mahabharata*, a virile hermit helps Vichitravirya's widows bear children without the intervention of a yagna or the gods. Later, the gods directly make Pandu's wives pregnant. What is magical (some would argue implicit) in the *Ramayana* is very explicit in the *Mahabharata*.

In both cases, celibate hermits and virile gods are called in to revive barren households. It is indeed a crisis of masculinity. Both Dasharatha and Shantanu are visualized as spent forces, of weak seed, who need the intervention of sages to restore royal virility. Thus, spiritual power replenishes material scarcity. The story seeks to make a case for the limitations of material power. The austerities of the sages contribute to the welfare of the kingdoms.

Both the *Ramayana* and the *Mahabharata* draw attention to how the austerities of forest ascetics rejuvenate the sapping strength of society, embodied in the inability of a king to secure a wife or father a child. Culture (sanskriti) is created when nature (prakriti) is domesticated. The village (grama) and the city (nagar) are the outcome of taming the woods (vana) and the forest (aranya).

Over time, the energy of the civilized world dwindles, as people indulge their sensory hunger (bhoga). This energy is replenished from the infinite reserve of nature via the tapasvis. They practised tapasya—restraining the senses (indriya), disciplining them, and not being overwhelmed by sensory inputs and temptations. This generates inner fire (tapa) that is used by kings to rejuvenate society—by invoking gods and enabling childless kings to be fathers.

10

Both celebrate obedient sons

In the Confucian world view of China, an orderly society is established when subjects submit to the will of kings, women to the will of men, the younger generation to the will of the older generation, and children to the will of their parents. So, all of civilized society makes obedience a virtue. The major religions of the world—Judaism, Christianity and Islam—also speak of how humans should follow the will of God, the creator of the world, revealed in the holy books through angels and prophets. Similarly, in the *Ramayana* and the *Mahabharata* too, which deal with kings and royal families, and property disputes, obedience is a virtue valued above all others—sons who obey their unreasonable fathers unconditionally are valorized.

But things are not so simple.

In the *Ramayana*, Ram gives up his claim to the throne and goes to the forest for fourteen years without remorse or regret. He does this to uphold the family reputation. Thus, he spends his youth in the forest, away from the power and pleasures of royal life, at the mercy of the elements. Again, after his return, he abandons his wife to protect the family reputation. His father's wish and the family reputation are given precedence over his own desires, making him the ideal son.

In the *Mahabharata*, Devavrata gives up his right to his father's throne and even his conjugal rights, so that his old father, Shantanu, can marry the fisherwoman, Satyavati. In this case, the father does not ask his son to give up anything, it is the son who cannot bear to see his father suffer. And so, the entire crisis in the epic hinges on the son's willingness to sacrifice his personal happiness for the father. By giving up his conjugal rights, Devavrata effectively prevents himself from fathering children, which means he will never repay his debt to the ancestors (pitr-rinn). This is a terrible vow (Bhishma, in Sanskrit), which is why Devavrata is henceforth called Bhishma, the one who takes the terrible vow that entraps him forever in 'put'—the hell reserved for childless men. He will never be able to escape this fate, as there is no offspring on earth to help him.

Both Ram and Bhishma give up their youth and the joys of life for the sake of their fathers and by doing so, they earn the respect of their families. Yet, it is Ram who is seen as the embodiment of divinity, not Bhishma. For Ram's motivation is not so much his father but Ayodhya. No one in the kingdom should doubt the integrity of the king and the royal family. In Bhishma's case, Hastinapur is not even the consideration. His sacrifice is to only satisfy the lust of his father. Hence, while Ram is venerated, Bhishma is pinned to the ground with arrows, and is forced to watch his family members kill each other.

The question being raised is the *intention* of the act of obedience, the thought behind the decision, the belief underlying the behaviour. Ram is more concerned about social stability—which depends on the kingdom trusting the royal family—than his father's pleasure and approval. For Bhishma, his father's pleasure and approval matter more than the stability of the kingdom.

Psychoanalysts speak of the Oedipus complex found in Greek mythology where a man unknowingly kills his father and marries his mother. It reflects a culture ridden with guilt, as the younger generations overpower the older generations. In Hindu mythology, psychoanalysts have found the very opposite—the Yayati complex, where the father prevails over the son; in other words, the son is overpowered by the will of the father. However, a deeper exploration reveals that the sons—Ram and Bhishma—let their respective father's will prevail. In Ram's case, this has a positive impact. In Bhishma's case, this has a negative impact. As Bhishma struggles to set right the damage caused by his decision, Krishna intervenes, pins him to the ground, and lets the world take its own course.

Ram succeeds in taking care of the whole world, at the cost of those closest to him. Bhishma, on the other hand, lets his kingdom suffer as he strives to bind his family together. That is why Ram is a god, and Bhishma, simply venerable, an elder with flaws.

Krishna, however, challenges father figures, much like the Greek heroes. He kills his maternal uncle, Kamsa, and Kamsa's father-in-law, Jarasandha, and later enables the Pandavas to kill their elders, including the patriarch Bhishma, the tutor Drona, the half-brother Karna and the uncle Shalya. Krishna brings the Greek way into the Indian world view, for the Indian world view is inclusive. It is this *and* that, not this *or* that.

11

Both speak of a shadowy sister, subservient twins and powerful maternal uncles

In some regional *Ramayanas*, Dasharatha has a daughter, Shanta, who is given away in adoption to Lomasha, and eventually, in marriage to Rishyashringa, who conducts the yagna that brings rain to the kingdom of Lomasha and sons to the household of Dasharatha. Nothing else is known about her.

Likewise, in the *Mahabharata*, the Pandavas have one cousin sister, Dushala. When Dhritarashtra's wife, Gandhari, delivers a ball of cold flesh instead of a baby, Vyasa offers to cut it into a hundred pieces and put them in pots to incubate them with the powers of mantra so that they transform into a hundred sons. 'Can I also have a daughter?' asks Gandhari. 'So be it,' says Vyasa and thus, Dushala is born—the only sister of the Kauravas. Not much is known about her except that her husband is Jayadhratha, who tries to molest Draupadi, and plays a key role in the killing of Arjuna's son by Subhadra, Abhimanyu.

In the *Ramayana*, Sumitra bears twins—Lakshman and Shatrughna—who are devoted to Ram and Bharat, respectively. In the *Mahabharata*, Madri bears twins—Nakula and Sahadeva—who are devoted to the sons of Kunti. The twins are content to live in the shadow of their illustrious older brothers.

In the *Ramayana*, Lakshman sets off a chain of events when he cuts Ravana's sister Surpanakha's nose. In the war to rescue Sita, he plays a key role when he kills Indrajit. Shatrughna plays a key role after Ram's coronation, when he fights Lavanasura. He also visits Valmiki's ashrama and meets the twin boys who are singing the epic of Ram. He then invites them to Ayodhya, not realizing they are Ram's sons.

Nakula and Sahadeva are known for their beauty and oracular powers, respectively. Nakula is described as vain, consumed by the attention women give him, and Sahadeva is silent, never revealing what he is aware of. But little else is known. Kunti's sons claim to never treat the twins as stepbrothers (they have different mothers but the same biological father). However, when it comes to gambling his possessions away, Yudhishthira gambles the twins first, before gambling Bhima or Arjuna (who have the same mother and father), revealing his real favourites. Later, Yudhishthira redeems himself during the exile when he asks that the twins be revived first at the poisoned lake of the crane, before asking for life to be breathed back into his brothers, Bhima and Arjuna.

In a large, extended family, there are distant relations who play a small but significant role in our lives. Perhaps that is what both epics are drawing our attention to when they talk of maternal uncles who interfere in family politics—Ashwapati in the *Ramayana*, and Shakuni as well as Vasudeva in the *Mahabharata*.

In the *Ramayana*, there is constant reference to Kaikeyi's family—her father Ashwapati of the Kekeya kingdom, and her brother Yudhajit. There are suggestions that the only reason she marries Dasharatha is because the childless king promises her father that even though Kaikeyi would be his junior queen, her son would be his heir. As luck would have it, it is the older queen,

Kaushalya, who bears the firstborn after Rishyashringa's yagna, causing confusion. A similar confusion arises in the *Mahabharata* when Gandhari, who becomes pregnant first, bears her hundred children after Kunti has given birth to her firstborn, Yudhishthira, with the help of the gods.

In the *Mahabharata*, the Kauravas are supported by their maternal uncle, Shakuni, king of Gandhara. The Pandavas have two mothers—Kunti, who is the mother of the elder trio and Madri, who is the mother of the younger twins. So, they have two maternal uncles—Vasudeva, brother of Kunti, and Shalya, brother of Madri. Vasudeva's son, Krishna, fights on the side of the Pandavas. Duryodhana manages to trick Shalya into fighting for the Kauravas.

12

Both speak of wives won as trophies in archery contests

In both the *Ramayana* and the *Mahabharata* there is reference to the swayamvara, a ceremony in which a woman selects her own husband. However, when the event is described, we realize that the woman in question never really chooses her husband. She is the trophy given to the winner of an archery contest.

In the *Ramayana*, Janaka offers the hand of Sita to the man who will string the bow of Shiva. No man can pick up the bow, let alone string it. Even Ravana tries and fails. When Ram picks the bow and breaks it while trying to string it, Janaka offers him the hand of Sita in marriage. One can't help wonder if the breaking rather than stringing of the bow foreshadows the future tragedy of separation which befalls the couple, as it indicates Ram's passion rather than Ram's equanimity. This is left unsaid.

In the *Mahabharata*, Arjuna is able to shoot the eye of a fish rotating on a wheel that is hanging from the ceiling just by looking at its reflection. This is how he wins the hand of Draupadi. She too, like Sita, is a trophy. However, Draupadi has some say in who can participate in the contest. In other words, she can create an eligibility criterion. She refuses to let Karna participate as he is the son of a charioteer. One wonders if this is the reason why Krishna does not participate, despite being present, for by disqualifying the foster son of a charioteer, Draupadi has effectively disqualified the foster son of a cowherd. This is also left unsaid.

Wives thus won are addressed by their father's name or the name of their father's kingdom. Sita is addressed as Janaki (Janaka's daughter), or Maithili (Mithila's princess) or Vaidehi (Videha's lady). Draupadi (Drupada's daughter) is also known as Panchali (Panchala's princess). Her mothers-in-law are called Kunti (Kuntibhoja's daughter), Madri (Madra's princess) and Gandhari (Gandhara's princess).

Sita is Sita's own name; likewise, Pritha is Kunti's personal name. Both names are linked to the earth—Sita means 'furrow', created in the earth by the hoe of the plough, and Pritha means earth-goddess, the responsibility of Prithu, the earth-king.

In the *Ramayana*, the sisters of Sita marry the brothers of Ram.

In the *Mahabharata*, Draupadi has no sister. Instead, Arjuna shares her with all his brothers.

The archery contest draws attention to the role the bow played in Vedic times. It is the weapon of the gods. A bow using Mount Meru as the shaft is used by Shiva to destroy the three worlds. A bow with sugarcane as the shaft is used by Kama to evoke desire in all creatures. The bow is a symbol of poise and balance—too tight and it will break, too loose and it is of no use. It embodies the dependable householder who engages with the world without seeking control over it, essentially how humans ought to conduct themselves—outgrowing our animal side, which is dominating and territorial and fearful and hungry, yet not becoming a hermit who is indifferent to the world itself.

13

Both speak of single parents

In the forest, there are different kinds of families. Amongst birds, both parents take care of the children. With tigers, it is the female who takes care of the litter. However, within society, we choose family structures. Both the *Ramayana* and the *Mahabharata* give great value to marriage, and family headed by a man who has one or many wives. Yet, both refer to single parents.

In the *Ramayana*, the female protagonist, Sita, raises her children, Luv and Kush, alone in the forest. In the *Mahabharata*, there are many such examples. Kunti raises the five Pandavas on her own after the death of her husband, Pandu. Hidimba raises Ghatotkacha on her own; Bhima plays no rule in his upbringing. Ulupi raises Aravan on her own; Arjuna plays no rule in his upbringing. Chitrangada raises Babruvahana on her own; Arjuna plays no rule in his upbringing. There is no taboo attached to single mothers raising children on their own.

We must not assume that child-rearing is bound to motherhood. In the *Mahabharata*, the apsara leaves her newborn, Shakuntala, on the forest ground and rises to heaven. The abandoned Shakuntala is found by Kanva, a rishi, who raises the child as his own. Thus, Kanva becomes the single father of an adopted child. Shakuntala also raises her child, Bharat, on her own, when Dushyanta refuses to acknowledge her as his wife.

Shantanu finds the abandoned twin children of a rishi called Sharadwana and an apsara called Janapadi, and adopts them. They are raised in his palace as Kripa and Kripi. He too is a single father of two adopted children.

The idea of a 'normal' family with one father, one mother and children is not imagined by either of the epics. Family is clearly seen as a place where children are nurtured with love, food and education. This love can also be provided by a single parent of either gender. This makes the two epics 'modern' by today's standards. But they were just accepting of diversity, which is the norm in the world. In fact, in nature, there is diversity in all matters. Only in culture, with nature domesticated and land cultivated, is diversity resisted and we seek to normalize things with a single dominant discourse.

14

Both refer to the power of faithful wives

Chastity and celibacy are not known in the forest. These are purely cultural imaginations. Hindu mythology speaks of chaste women and celibate men—mirror images of each other. What a woman acquires through chastity, a man acquires through celibacy—a power that makes the woman a sati and the man a siddha. This power is seen as heat and light locked in the body, which can be summoned at will. It is tapa, or fire, that does not need fuel.

Sati is both a proper noun and a common noun in the scriptures. As a proper noun, it is the name of Daksha's daughter who immolated herself, as she could not bear how her venerable father insulted her beloved husband, Shiva. As a common noun, it refers to a faithful wife, whose chastity gives her magical powers, like the ability to withstand the heat of fire. This latter concept plays an important role in both the *Ramayana* and the *Mahabharata*. In medieval times, the word 'sati' was used to refer to widows who burned themselves on their husband's funeral pyre, a practice that has long been banned under Indian law. People often confuse these three concepts.

In the *Ramayana*, Sita is a sati, or chaste wife. She is faithful to Ram, and does not look at other men. And so, she has the power to withstand the strength of the flames and prove her chastity to all. This story of Sita is foreshadowed by two tales of female infidelity. The first involves Renuka, wife of Jamadagni, who briefly desires a man, for which transgressive thought she loses her sati powers that enabled her to collect water from the river in unbaked pots made from river clay. She is beheaded, on the orders of her husband, by her own son, Parashurama. The second story involves Ahalya who is turned to stone by her husband, the sage Gautama, who discovers her in bed with Indra. We are not sure if Ahalya was tricked into bed by Indra, or if she was a willing participant. Thus, Renuka is contaminated by thought while Ahalya is contaminated by action. In Sita's case, she is pure in thought and action, but contaminated by reputation, which is why Ram abandons her. The concept of sati has been used in traditional Hindu society to domesticate women and reinforce patriarchy.

In the *Mahabharata*, Gandhari shares her husband's blindness by blindfolding herself. Thus, she gets sati powers. When she removes her blindfold, her glance holds so much power that it can make her son's body impervious to weapons. To prevent this from happening, Krishna tricks Duryodhana into wearing some leaves and covering his loins, so that a part of his body remains vulnerable. Gandhari's angry glance, following the death of her sons, turns Yudhishthira's toe black. She also has the power to curse Krishna. Her curse is realized when Krishna witnesses his family members killing each other in a civil war, and when he himself is shot dead by a hunter.

We are told that Draupadi is also a sati despite having five husbands, because she passes through fire and makes herself pure each time she completes a year with one husband. She then prepares for her visit to the next husband. No such demand is placed on the men with multiple wives, reminding us how the concept of sati is used to control and rein in women. In Tamil versions of the *Mahabharata*, in the ritual where Draupadi is acknowledged as a goddess, we are told that after the war, women on both sides are asked to walk through fire. Draupadi walks through fire unscathed, but the widows of the Kauravas are consumed by the flames—perhaps to demonstrate that, unlike Draupadi, they are not chaste enough to protect their husbands; or perhaps to rid the world of all things linked to the villainous Kauravas so the Pandavas can start afresh.

Valmiki's *Ramayana* does not refer to the practice of widows burning themselves on the husband's funeral pyre. The widows of Dasharatha do not commit sati. And the widows of Vali, the monkey-king, and Ravana, the demon-king, Tara and Mandodari, marry the younger brothers, Sugriva and Vibhishana, of their respective husbands. In fact, in the *Rig Veda*, there is a hymn where the widow is first asked to lie down next to the body of her dead husband and then asked to get up holding the hand of her husband's living kin, indicating that she is being welcomed back into the world of the living after being her husband's partner till his death. This hymn was arguably misinterpreted and misused to get widows killed after their husbands died so that they could not claim the husband's property after his death. While some of Krishna's wives commit sati after he dies, others simply become nuns. The widows of the Kaurava warriors slain at Kurukshetra do not commit sati either. It was clearly not a mandatory practice, at best a misguided voluntary practice, based on the assumption that women have no life after their husbands' death.

It is important to ask why men were expected to be celibate, and not chaste. And why women were expected to be chaste, not celibate. This has to do with nature. Nature does not need all males of a species—only one or two to make the females pregnant to produce the next generation. Nature values every female greatly—as it is in her womb that the next generation is created—but it does not value all males, just the strongest and the fittest.

By recommending that most men be celibate, culture was ensuring that mediocre men let the more worthy men father the next generation. In exchange, they were being offered magical powers and freedom from household responsibilities. The more worthy men were encouraged to have many wives, an idea that Ram resists, as he insists on being ekam-patni-vrata—the man with only one wife—for he is fully committed to Sita. He also keeps a golden statue of her beside him and refuses to replace her with another queen when he is forced to abandon her.

This can be seen as a kind of social engineering in ancient times. If every woman became celibate, where would children come from? By asking a woman to be chaste, society can be certain of who the father is, and this information is important in inheritance issues, indicating how the chastity of women is closely linked to patriarchy. In exchange for submission to these rules of domestication, women were promised magical powers. Of course, if the husband died before the wife, she was deemed responsible for this ill fortune and aspersions were cast on her, like not having been 'chaste' enough to protect her man. So, to prove their chastity, women were asked to kill themselves on the funeral pyre. With the wife/daughter-in-law out of the way, the family could regain control of her husband's wealth and land. But there were women who saw through this scheme; Kunti refuses to kill herself when Pandu dies, as Madri does, thereby ensuring that her sons get their rightful share of the Kuru inheritance.

15

Both have supernatural heroines

Sita, the female protagonist of the *Ramayana*, is born from the earth. Draupadi, the female protagonist of the *Mahabahrata*, is born out of fire. Thus, both have supernatural births, like the male leads. But while Ram and the Pandavas owe their existence to the devas, gods who live in the celestial regions, Sita and Draupadi are firmly earthbound, reinforcing their association with the Goddess.

In Vedic mythology, the sky is the father and the earth is the mother, separated by Indra, which reflects the sky-association of the epic heroes and the earth-association of the epic heroines.

In the *Ramayana*, Janaka, the king of Videha, ploughs Sita out while conducting the ritual sowing ceremony with a golden plough. In some narrations, the earth-goddess herself emerges and gives Sita to the childless Janaka. In later regional narrations, she is the daughter of Mandodari, wife of Ravana, who is cast into the sea and rescued by the sea-god who gives her to the earth-goddess, who in turn gives her to Janaka.

In the *Mahabharata*, Drupada, king of Panchala, invites Yaja and Upayaja to perform a yagna that will give him a child. When the yagna is complete, and the magic potion is ready, the queen is called. But at that moment she is busy bathing, so the priests throw the magic potion in the fire and from the sacrificial pit appear a pair of fully grown twins, a boy and a girl—named Dhrishtadyumna and Draupadi.

That Sita and Draupadi are not mere heroines but supernatural beings, perhaps manifestations of the Goddess, is also suggested by their hair! Traditionally, when the Goddess is wild and bloodthirsty, her hair is unbound. However, when she is domestic and nurturing, her hair is tied with flowers and jewellery. Bound hair means civilization is regulated; unbound hair means the end of civilization and a return to nature, where sex and violence are unregulated.

In the *Ramayana*, when Ravana abducts Sita, she drops all her jewellery so that it marks a trail that will enable Ram to find her. When Hanuman visits her, she gives him the final piece of jewellery she still has with her—her hairpin (chudamani)—to give to Ram, suggesting that she is at the end of her tether. She is ready to turn into Kali, unless Ram overpowers Ravana, who does not respect the rules of marriage, thereby not respecting culture.

In the *Mahabharata*, after she is publicly humiliated by the Kauravas, Draupadi swears not to tie her hair until she washes it with Kaurava blood. Thus, she evokes Kali in her vengeance. In Tamil versions of the epic, she declares she will wash her hair with Kaurava blood, comb it with Kaurava bones, tie it with Kaurava entrails, and decorate it with Kaurava hearts.

16

Both value education and gurus

In hero myths around the world, the hero has a mentor or a teacher, who prepares him for the heroic journey in his destiny. This is part of the 'monomyth' theory that is very popular in Hollywood, according to which all stories in the world are essentially heroic narratives where a young woman or man goes on a quest during which s/he transforms the world and is transformed themself. Enabling them in this process is a wise old man; for example, Merlin the magician guides King Arthur of Avalon.

The *Ramayana* and the *Mahabharata* do not fit into the standard Western monomyth template. Ram and the Pandavas are not quite heroes on a heroic quest, though many scholars insist on seeing them through this narrow lens. But both Ram and Pandavas do have mentors in their lives. These mentors are called acharyas (those who teach skills), and gurus (those who expand one's perspective of the world). Many of them are rishis (seers with a deep insight of the world within and without), who live in the forest as hermits, and to whose hermitages kings send their sons for training. In the *Ramayana*, the gurus of Ram are Vasistha and Vishwamitra. Ram's sons are educated by Valmiki. In the *Mahabharata*, the gurus of the Pandavas are Kripa, then Drona, and eventually, Krishna. There is Parashurama, who is the guru of the Kaurava generals, Bhishma, Drona and Karna. In the *Bhagavata*, we learn that Krishna also has a guru called Sandipani.

Ram is sent to the Vasishtha's ashrama where he is trains to fulfil his destiny as the future king, as he is the eldest son of the royal family. In a tradition that came about much later, we are told that Ram, after his education, goes on a pilgrimage and returns wondering if life has a purpose. He also expresses his desire to become a hermit. This is when Vasishtha tells him stories, compiled in the *Yoga Vasishtha*, that essentially teach him how to live like a householder but with the mind of a hermit. Thus, Ram is transformed into the householder-hermit which was seen in Hindu philosophy as greater than both the unenlightened householder and the enlightened hermit.

In the *Valmiki Ramayana*, however, Ram has another teacher—Vishwamitra. Stories of rivalry between Vasishtha and Vishwamitra are part of Puranic lore. Vasishtha is one of the seven celestial sages, and so, is essentially a sage by birth. By contrast, Vishwamitra is a king who becomes a sage through austerities. The tension between the two reveals the conflict between the sages and the kings of Vedic times. The tension was mainly over who had more influence—the one with access to spiritual knowledge or the one with control over the material realm.

A similar tension is revealed in the education of Ram, imparted by Vasishtha and Vishwamitra, where Vasishtha is seen as providing Vedic knowledge—including knowledge of celestial mantra-charged weapons—to Ram in the safety of a hermitage, while Vishwamitra drags Ram to the forest, much against the king's wishes and gives him practical knowledge, which includes knowing how to forgive the adultress Ahalya who has been rejected by her own husband, how to kill Tadaka even though she is a woman, and finally, how to find a wife by winning an archery contest in Mithila. Vishwamitra also narrates stories of Ram's royal ancestors—how one of them, Bhagiratha, got River Ganga to descend from heaven to earth and how another one, Sagar, was responsible for establishing the sea! Thus, Vishwamitra's education seems more practical while Vasistha's is more theoretical. Later in the epic, Ram's children are raised in the forest in the hermitage of Valmiki, who teaches them to sing the *Ramayana* and also trains them to be warriors who can stop Ram's royal horse and challenge his army. The education is clearly holistic, involving aesthetics and the arts, as well as military skills. A good king is thus not just a warrior but one who also appreciates the arts.

In the *Mahabharata*, the gurus lack the nobility of the gurus in the *Ramayana*. They train the royals to be great warriors but there is not much education on aesthetics and dharma. Parashurama trains Bhishma, Drona, and even Karna, but curses Karna that he will forget all he has learnt when he needs the knowledge the most as Karna lies about his family roots. Parashurama tells Drona not to share his knowledge with warrior families but Drona does exactly that, offering his services to the Kuru royal family in exchange for a fee. Drona trains his students but favours Arjuna and his son, and discriminates against Karna and Ekalavya. Lessons in humility are taught to Pandavas not by Drona, but later in the forest, by Shiva, in the form of a tribal man (Kirata) and Hanuman in the form of an old monkey. Krishna is taught the Vedic way by Sandipani but greater attention is given to the fee that Krishna pays Sandipani—he brings back Sandipani's dead son to the land of the living, a supernatural feat that establishes Krishna as a divine being. Later, in the Kurukshetra, Krishna presents the Bhagavad Gita to Arjuna. Here, Vedic wisdom—

what it means to be a hermit-householder—is transmitted to the Pandava, Arjuna; a knowledge that Parashurama and Drona and Kripa seem to have failed to transmit to the warring princes of the Kuru family.

III

Rupture

In which we discover predisposing karmic factors and very similar precipitating aspects that cause the crisis and take the story forward.

17

Both presuppose a crisis of kingship

Parashurama exists in the background of the two epics. We are told that with his axe he rids the earth of kings. Why? Because the kings have burdened the earth with their greed and they exploit the earth instead of maintaining a balance between nature and culture. In other words, they follow adharma (using kingship to corner wealth and power for personal use) rather than raj dharma (using kingship to create an ecosystem of security where economy thrives). They break the promise made to the earth-cow, gau-mata, by the first king of the earth, Prithu. The trigger for the killings is the Haihaiya king, Kartaviryarjuna.

Kartavirya desires a cow that belongs to Parashurama's father, Jamadagni. He tries to take it by force. Parashurama stops him and in the duel that follows, Parashurama uses his axe to hack the king to pieces. This triggers a crisis. Kartavirya's sons attack and kill Jamadagni, and burn his hermitage down. Disgusted by the arrogance of kings, Parashurama kills not only Kartavirya's sons but all the kings of the earth. He fills five great lakes with their blood.

A new crop of kings emerge whose stories are told in the *Ramayana* and *Mahabharata*. The new kings, we are told, are born when the royal widows invite Brahmins to make them pregnant. Thus, the violent bloodline of kings is purified by the seed of non-violent Brahmin sages. This thought is subtly implied in the *Ramayana*, when Dasharatha's children are born with the help of Rishyashringa. In the *Mahabharata*, this is more explicit when Vyasa is called upon to impregnate the widows of Vichitravirya.

Parashurama makes his presence felt in both the epics. In the *Ramayana*, when Ram breaks Shiva's bow, Parashurama appears and challenges him to pick up Vishnu's bow. In different retellings, he is either overpowered or overwhelmed by Ram, for in Ram he discovers hope—a Kshatriya who is the very embodiment of dharma.

In the *Mahabharata*, the three commanders of the Kaurava army—Bhishma, Drona and Karna—are his students. He trains them in warfare but they still follow the path of adharma by taking the side of a man who refuses to part with the land which belongs to his cousins. Krishna orchestrates the killing of these three commanders. In other words, what Parashurama creates, Krishna destroys.

Thus, the two epics can be seen as epics of kings who rose in the post-Parashurama era, restoring faith in the Kshatriyas who were tainted by the misdeeds of Kartavirya.

Historians have pointed out that the rise of the maha-janapadas in the time of the Buddha marks the shift from kinship (groups bound by blood or marriage) to kingship (rise of a king who towers over multiple, unrelated clans, communities, and tribes). This is when people started asking questions as to what constitutes a good king. The idea of raj dharma started being discussed in the Dharma-shastras. A good king valued atma gyan, and did not indulge his aham. Indulgence of aham made kings envious of other people's prosperity, making them covet others' cows, like Kartavirya, for instance, or other people's wives, like Ravana, and other people's land, like Duryodhana.

18

Both deal with enchanting, ambitious queens

In the Vedas, we find ritual expression of desire. The gods are invoked, praised with song, offered food, and then asked for favours—cows, horses, children, grain and gold. But as we have seen, the Buddha declared desire as the cause of all suffering. When we get what we want we get addicted, when we don't get what we want we get frustrated.

Over time, sexual desire came to be seen as a negative force. In Buddhism, it was personified as Mara, the demon of desire, and his daughters. In Hinduism, it was Kama, god of desire, and his legion of nymphs, the apsaras, who Shiva burns with his third eye.

Both the *Ramayana* and the *Mahabharata* attribute a man's desire for a woman, and a woman's desire for power and property, as the cause of all misfortune. In the *Ramayana*, it is the love of Dasharatha for the ambitious Kaikeyi that triggers a crisis, while in the *Mahabharata*, it is the love of Shantanu for the ambitious Satyavati that leads to a chain of disastrous events.

Dasharatha loves Kaikeyi very much, and as gratitude for saving his life in the battlefield, he offers her two boons. So, on the eve of Ram's coronation, she asks that Ram be sent into forest exile and her son, Bharat, be crowned king instead.

Shantanu wants to marry Satyavati, but her father wants him to assure her that her children will be Shantanu's royal heirs. Although Shantanu's son agrees to give up his right to the throne and his right to marry and start a family, just so that his old father can marry a young fisherwoman, the stage is set for future disaster. Satyavati's sons are weaklings, and their progeny are disabled, ultimately giving rise to the Kauravas and Pandavas who go to war.

In both stories, the problem is with the second queen, who is described as beautiful, sensual and alluring. Dasharatha marries Kaikeyi because his first queen, Kaushalya, is not able to give him a child and he has heard from astrologers that Kaikeyi is destined to bear sons. Shantanu's first wife is the river-goddess, Ganga, who leaves him when he questions her actions after marriage, breaking the vow he had made to her. His second wife, Satyavati, is gifted with a bodily fragrance that makes her irresistible to men.

Both Kaikeyi and Satyavati are shown as highly independent queens. Kaikeyi joins her husband in battle and saves his life, thus earning the two boons. Satyavati ferries pilgrims across the river and earns the attention of a sage called Parasara who gets rid of her fishy odour and makes her body fragrant after she agrees to bear him a child.

Desire for pleasure, power and property triggers the crisis in both the epics. Such desires exist only in humans. In animals, the primal desire is hunger. Animals constantly seek food. They hoard only for a season. But, in humans, hunger is insatiable and there is no limit to our desire to hoard. This is because our imagination conjures up situations of eventual calamity and scarcity, thus consuming us. An uncontrolled mind attains a completely self-indulgent state, where we are so consumed by our hungers, fears and desires that we ignore others, or see them as mere tools to achieve our ends. How does one prevent this?

The hermit way is to meditate and move inwards, stripping our mind of imaginary situations and focusing on reality over fantasy. But this results in a state of absolute indifference, where we disconnect from all external relationships, and feel neither emotions nor sensations. So the *Ramayana* and the *Mahabharata* came up with a different option—where we focus on the desires of the larger ecosystem over our own.

Dasharatha has to decide what matters more—his wife's desire, or the wishes of his subjects. Shantanu too has to decide what matters more—his wife's desire, or the wishes of his subjects. What is the dharma of a king? What is the dharma of a husband? Are they first husbands or kings?

This dilemma has repercussions later in the narrative. What matters more? Sita's desire for her husband's support, or the desire of Ayodha's residents to get rid of a queen of soiled reputation? Draupadi's desire for vengeance, or every attempt to make peace with the Kauravas? The personal and professional crises give rise to ethical and moral dilemmas, called dharma-sankat.

19

Both draw attention to violence against women

In the *Ramayana*, violence against women is a consistent theme. Ram is encouraged to kill the rakshasa-woman, Tadaka. But is not stri-hatya (killing of women) disallowed, wonders Ram, remembering the teachings of Vasishtha. Vishwamitra insists that Ram shoot his arrow and kill Tadaka. Later, Ram encounters Ahalya, turned into stone by her husband, Gautama, for her infidelity. Ram liberates Ahalya from the curse. Violence is directed at the maid, Manthara, who poisons Kaikeyi's mind and gets Kaikeyi to demand Ram's exile and Bharat's coronation. Then, in the forest, Lakshman cuts the nose and ears of Surpanakha, a brutal punishment as she persistently makes sexual advances towards him and Ram, threatening to hurt Sita who she sees as a rival. Ravana is furious when he learns of the disfigurement of his sister, and instead of attacking Ram, he abducts Sita and holds her captive in his island-kingdom of Lanka. While travelling over the sea, Ram's messenger, Hanuman, overpowers many female demons—such as Surasa, Simhika and Lankini—who guard Ravana's citadel. In visual depictions, Hanuman is sometimes shown trampling a woman, Panoti, the demon of malevolent astrological forces.

While the violence against women in the *Ramayana* is

predominantly against rakshasa-women, in the *Mahabharata*, the violence is within the family. Amba, Ambika and Ambalika are abducted and forced to marry men they do not want. Gandhari blindfolds herself to share her husband's blindness. But all this pales when compared to the violence Draupadi, the common wife of the five Pandavas, is subjected to. She is abused thrice. The first time is when Yudhishthira gambles her away and Dusshasana grabs her by the hair, drags her to the assembly hall and tries to disrobe her in public. The second time is when during the forest exile, finding her alone in the house, Jayadhrata tries to abduct her. And finally, while hiding in Virata's palace as the queen's maid, she has to face the sexual advances and the violence of the queen's brother, Kichaka. When Kichaka is killed, his brothers try to burn Draupadi alive.

One often points to these stories to explain the low status of women in India. But this is not quite accurate. Both the *Ramayana* and the *Mahabharata* show women who demand their husband keep their promise—in the *Ramayana*, Kaikeyi demands Dasharatha give her the boons he promised her, while in the *Mahabharata*, both Ganga and Satyavati refuse to marry Shantanu until he agrees to their conditions.

Sita, too, is shown as having agency when she makes choices on her own—the decision to accompany Ram to the forest, the personal risk of feeding the hungry hermit who turns out to be Ravana, turning down Hanuman's plan to escape Lanka by riding on his shoulders, accompanying Ram back to Ayodhya, and finally, the decision to renounce her family and return to her mother's abode. Draupadi also displays agency when she chooses to not let Karna compete for her hand in marriage, when she challenges the rules that let her be gambled away by her husband, when she refuses to tie her hair until she has washed it with the blood of the Kauravas, and when she demands that the jewel of Ashwathama be wrenched from his skull. Sita responds silently; Draupadi speaks her mind.

While many scholars like to point out the misogyny and patriarchy of the Hindu epics, it is important to compare and contrast it with the misogyny and patriarchy found in mythologies from other parts of the world. In the Bible, one often comes across lines where God tells his Chosen People to attack tribes of those who worship 'false gods' and kill every man, woman and child. In the Greek epics, Greek soldiers rape Trojan women after their victory at Troy and turn them into concubines. In fact, this ill treatment of women of the vanquished by victors is absent in the Hindu epics. After Ram's victory, the wives of Ravana and the women of Lanka are treated with respect. After the Pandava victory, the Kaurava widows are not raped or enslaved.

Buddhism and Jainism frown on all kinds of violence, but both consider the female biology inadequate to attain liberation from the cycle of birth and death. Abandonment of wives by sages in the pursuit of enlightenment is a key feature of both Buddhist and Jain lore. By contrast, the *Ramayana* and the *Mahabharata* see women as integral to the narrative. There can be no *Ramayana* without Sita, no *Mahabharata* without Draupadi. It is as much their story, as it the story of Ram and Krishna.

20

Both have secret stories of vengeance

The regional and folk *Ramayanas* and *Mahabharatas*, which started being put down in writing less than a thousand years ago, have many stories that are not found in the classical Sanskrit retelling. Are these stories variants? Are they innovations? Are they stories that were kept out by the Sanskrit composers? We can only speculate. But they give the epics an entirely new spin.

In the folk retelling of the *Ramayana*, especially in shadow puppet theatres of Tamil Nadu, Karnataka, Andhra Pradesh and Kerala, we are told that Surpanakha initiated the war between Ram and Ravana. It so happened that once she wanted to eat meat that her sister-in-law—Ravana's wife Mandodari—would not serve her. This led to an argument between Surpanakha's husband, Vidyutjihva, and her brother. Things got so out of control that Vidyutjihva opened his mouth, let out his lightning tongue and swallowed Ravana whole. From inside her husband's stomach, Ravana called out to Surpanakha and begged her to save him. But this entailed ripping her brother out from her husband's stomach. 'If you sacrifice your husband, I promise to make your son my heir to the throne of Lanka,' said the crafty Ravana. A gullible Surpanakha believed him, but soon realized she had been tricked. Sambukumar, Surpanakha's son, decided to avenge his father's death by invoking the gods and securing from them a sword that would help him kill Ravana. Unfortunately, just when the sword materialized, Lakshman stumbled upon it and saw it floating in the air. He swung it, and accidentally killed Sambukumar, to whom the sword actually belonged. Surpanakha was looking for her son's murderer when she spotted Ram. She realized that he had the power to defeat and kill Ravana—the cause of her misfortune. She tried to entice him with her charms but when her nose got cut, she used her humiliation to ignite a war with Ravana.

In the folk retelling of the *Mahabharata*, especially in the Odia *Mahabharata*, we hear how Shakuni plotted Kauravas' destruction by goading them to fight the Pandavas. After the birth of the Kauravas, Bhishma learns that their mother was a widow at the time of her marriage. It was foretold that Gandhari's second husband would be a king and give her great sons, so the king of Gandhara got her married to a goat that was immediately killed, which technically made Gandhari a widow, and Dhritarashtra her second husband. Fearing scandal, Bhishma decided to kill everyone who knew this secret. So he invited the king of Gandhara and his hundred sons to a meal and then locked them up and gave them only one portion of food every day, thus slowly starving them to death. Technically, Bhishma was not breaking the rules of hospitality—because he was offering them food. The king of Gandhara decided to feed only his youngest and smartest child, Shakuni, so that he would survive and avenge this treachery. To ensure that he never forgot, the king cut Shakuni's ankle, giving him a permanent limp. He also told his son, 'When I die, take the bones of my hand and turn them into dice. They will roll whichever way you wish. They will help you in plotting your revenge.' This was why Shakuni never let the Kauravas and Pandavas become friends. He kept the fires of jealousy burning between the cousins. It was his father's bones that ensured that the Pandavas lost the gambling match, leading to events that culminated in the great war between the Kauravas and the Pandavas, destroying the Kuru household. In alternative versions of the story, Shakuni's ire is directed not against Bhishma but against Duryodhana, who kills his own grandfather to protect his reputation.

In these stories, the lines between villains and heroes get blurred. Surpanakha and Shakuni turn out to be master strategists, pulling the strings from the background— the villains are actually victims of their own advisers. Surpanakha wants Ram to kill Ravana although she pretends Ram is the enemy. Likewise, Shakuni wants the Pandavas to defeat the Kauravas although he pretends to support the Kauravas. This idea of complex causality is a key theme in Hindu epics. The limited mind of humans does not understand the limitless and complex workings of karma.

21

Both deal with overconfident hunters
of frightened deer

Ancient India was known as Arya-varta, or the land of the noble
people. In the early scriptures, the region is described as the
land of seven mountains and seven rivers, where the black buck
roamed. Hunting deer was the favourite pastime of kings in Vedic
times. The rishis often used deerskin as clothing, and as mats to
sit and sleep on.

With the rise of the doctrine of ahimsa or non-violence,
hunting of deer for sport came to be frowned upon. And so, in
the *Ramayana*, Sita requests Ram not to hunt deer for sport,
and Ram argues that it is the hobby and habit of kings. In the
Mahabharata, the Pandavas leave the Dvaita forest and return to
the Kamyak forest after the deer there appear in Yudhishthira's
dream and complain that excessive hunting by the Pandavas is
causing their population to decline.

Deer contribute to many crises in the epics. In the *Ramayana*,
Sita is drawn to a dazzling, golden deer and asks Ram to fetch
it for her—dead or alive. Her desire for the deer is indicative of
forthcoming trouble because, as the Buddha declared, desire is
the cause of suffering. The deer turns out to be a shape-shifting
rakshasa, Marichi, who draws Ram, and eventually Lakshman,

away from Sita, enabling Ravana to kidnap her.

In the *Mahabharata*, the arani sticks—used to churn the sacred fire during the yagna—of a hermit get entangled in the antlers of a deer. The Pandavas go in search of the deer, and during this hunt, encounter the poisoned lake of the crane. The crane, who is the guardian of the lake, tells the Pandavas to answer his questions before taking a sip of the water; but the entitled Pandavas do not listen to the crane and decide to drink the water first. As a result, Nakula, Sahadeva, Arjuna and Bhima die. Yudhishthira, however, answers all the questions, and is able to save his brothers. The crane, and the deer, turn out to be Dharma, or Yama— Yudhishithira's celestial father.

Overconfident hunters in the two epics trigger a crisis. In the *Ramayana*, it is Ram's father, Dasharatha. In the *Mahabharata*, it is Pandu, the father of the Pandavas.

Dasharatha goes hunting and shoots an arrow when he hears the sound of what he believes is a deer drinking water. Great hunters are supposed to shoot simply by hearing the target, rather than seeing and then aiming for it. Instead of a deer, he strikes a youth collecting water from a river in a pot. This is Shravan Kumar, the ideal son. When Shravan's old, blind parents learn what Dasharatha has done, they curse him that he will die from the pain that follows when a parent loses their child. The curse manifests itself when Ram goes into forest exile and Dasharatha dies of heartbreak.

Pandu goes hunting and shoots an arrow at two deer that are mating. The arrow strikes them both. The deer turn out to be a sage called Kindama and his wife, who had taken the form of the animal to enjoy lovemaking in the open. Kindama curses Pandu that he will die the instant he tries to make love to his wife.

Realizing that he cannot father a child, and knowing that such 'disabled' men cannot be kings, Pandu renounces the throne and becomes a hermit, refusing to return to his city, and thus triggering a crisis. His blind elder brother becomes king in his place and Pandu's wives rush to the forest to give him company. Kunti, his elder wife, tells him of a law that enables men to father children if they are incapable of going to their wives. It is called niyoga. She also tells him she has the power to summon a god and have a child by him, if Pandu permits. Pandu gives Kunti permission to call three gods and have three sons by them—Yudhishthira from Indra, Bhima from Vayu and Arjuna from Indra. Madri calls upon the Ashwini twins and they give her the twins Nakula and Sahadeva. Pandu, thus, becomes the father of five sons without making love to any of his wives. Alas, one day, he cannot help but make love to Madri, and dies instantly. In sorrow, Madri kills herself on his funeral pyre and Kunti is left to raise the five sons of Pandu on her own.

In the Vedic texts, the deer becomes a metaphor for the restless mind that is pinned to the sky by Rudra, the Vedic form of Shiva. Poets used the deer to symbolize our desires, and the hunting of the deer as a metaphor for yoga, with the bow and arrow representing simultaneous balance and focus. But the overconfident hunters of the epics are hardly yogis, and the deer they hunt often turn out to be trouble in disguise.

IV

Exile

In which we realize how important the forest and its residents are to the stories as well as to the larger Indian philosophy.

22

Both speak of forest exile

The forest (vana, aranya) is an important backdrop in both the *Ramayana* and the *Mahabharata*. In fact, appreciating the forest as a space is key to understanding Hindu philosophy.

In the forest, there are no rules, no duties, no obligations. Everyone is driven by instinct. The strong, smart and nimble survive. The unfit perish. No one comes to anyone's help. This is the space of 'fish justice', i.e. matsya nyaya, where the big fish eat the small fish, and that is okay. This means, in society, this is not acceptable. In society, the mighty have to take care of the meek. Resources have to be made available for the unfit, and the weak. This is dharma for humans. When humans behave like animals, it is adharma. Animals are supposed to behave like animals, as they are hardwired to do so, but humans have a choice. In this choice is embedded the idea of dharma. The more human we are, the more we care for others, the more we walk on the path of dharma that takes us towards the divine.

The germ of this idea of separation of forest and field comes in the *Sama Veda*, where songs are classified as those to be sung in the forest and those to be sung in the settlement. The first is the wild, undomesticated, uncultivated, and unregulated space of nature (prakriti). The latter is the domesticated, cultivated, regulated, and controlled space of culture (sanskriti).

In the *Vishnu Purana*, the first avatar of Vishnu is a fish, thus alluding to matsya nyaya. This is reinforced when he approaches Manu while he is taking his bath in a river to 'save him from the big fish'. Manu provides the fish a pot of water to live in, but as the fish keeps growing in size, Manu has to keep providing him with larger and larger pots, until, finally, the fish is so big that even the sea is not enough to contain him. The rains that follow to make the sea larger, so as to accommodate the fish, end up drowning the earth. Manu is then saved by the big fish. This is how he learns the importance of culture as a space where the weak can thrive.

But this is also a tale of caution—excessive generosity is dangerous. Even when the fish gets big enough to take care of itself, Manu continues to provide for it, thus causing an imbalance in the ecosystem, resulting in the great deluge. Having turned into a big fish, the small fish now returns the favour and turns into Manu's saviour.

So, the tension between forest and settlement, nature and culture, is at the heart of Hindu philosophy. The forest is the place for tribes and hermits; the settlement is for householders. The raw elemental nature of the forest makes it a dangerous place, but also a place of liberation and wisdom, as it is not fettered by man-made rules.

In the *Ramayana*, Ram encounters the forest three times.

- First, he enters as a student, with Vishwamitra. This is when he encounters Tadaka and Ahalya.

- The second time, Ram enters the forest as an exile who, although accompanied by his wife, has to live like a hermit. This is when he encounters the vanaras and the rakshasas.

- The third time, Ram enters the forest as a king, following his horse as part of the royal land-claiming yagna. This is when he meets Sita, whom he had banished long ago from Ayodhya, and who, when asked to return home, refuses.

In the *Mahabharata*, the Pandavas encounter the forest six times.

- They are born in the forest.
- They return as refugees when the Kauravas set fire to their house.
- They return as city-builders, after they secure the forest of Khandava as inheritance, and build on it the city of Indraprastha.
- They are back in the forest for their exile after they gamble away their kingdom.
- The fifth time, they enter as kings, following their horse as part of the royal land-claiming yagna.
- Finally, they return to the forest a sixth time as hermits, after passing on the reins of the kingdom to their heir, Parikshit.

In both the *Ramayana* and *Mahabharata*, we are left to wonder which space is crueller—the forest or the human settlement. The whole point of culture is to create a space where the meek are taken care of by the mighty. Yet, this does not necessarily happen.

In the *Ramayana*, a woman's ambition results in her stepson being told to leave the security of the city and live in the forest for fourteen years. Later, public gossip results in a king abandoning his wife in the forest. In the *Mahabharata*, cousins set fire to the house of the Pandavas, forcing them to take refuge in the forest. In Hastinapur, a woman is dragged by the hair and publicly abused, and eventually the Pandavas and the Kauravas fight over land like dogs fighting over meat.

Thus, we are drawn from the physical world (forest) into the psychological world (animal mind). You can take humans out of the forest, but can you take the animal out of the human? For like animals, even in a village, humans can be territorial and dominating—fearful of rivals.

23

Both differentiate kitchen food from forest food

In the forest, there are no kitchens. Animals and plants do not cook their food. Humans do. The kitchen is a marker of culture. The kitchen fire is then the first yagna. In Ayodhya, Sita's kitchen (Sita ki rasoi) is a popular pilgrim spot. In the *Mahabharata*, reference is made to Draupadi's plate (Draupadi ki thali), which is always overflowing with food. Thus, the heroines of the two epics are closely related to culinary skills. Yet, in the forest, they encounter the food of the sages—uncooked tubers, fruits and berries.

At the heart of Hindu philosophy is the idea of food (anna), which when consumed becomes flesh (anna-kosha), and the body, which is the vehicle of the soul (atma). Feeding the body and keeping it healthy is the primary obligation (dharma) of a living creature. Nature is the source of food. Nature is the goddess. She is food. She is flesh. Flesh becomes food and food becomes flesh. Without the goddess there can be no sustenance, hence, without her, there can be no life. Wild food is processed in a kitchen. The kitchen (rasoi) is a sacred place where juices and flavours (rasa) are harnessed, and food (bhog) is prepared from grains, cereals, fruit, vegetables, fish and meat. The goddess, who is the forest, is also the goddess of the kitchen—Anna-poorna.

Shiva, the hermit-god, outgrows hunger, but then he notices

the hunger of his followers (ganas) and realizes that even if he does not need food, his followers do. This is how he learns to respect his wife—the kitchen goddess. This Puranic theme of respecting the kitchen manifests in the kitchens of Sita and Draupadi in the *Ramayana* and the *Mahabharata*, respectively.

In the *Ramayana*, Ravana gets Sita to leave the security of her hut by begging for food. To feed the hungry is the hallmark of nobility. Sita risks personal security to feed a stranger. In a folklore from Himachal, a crow takes a roti from Sita's kitchen and drops it in Lanka. When Ravana eats this roti he falls in love with the cook and travels the world looking for her, and finally ends up finding Sita.

In the *Mahabharata*, Draupadi, who is famous for feeding all who visit her, wonders how she will continue to feed those who come to her during the forest exile. So, Surya, the sun-god, gives her a vessel that overflows with food until Draupadi has had her meal. And so, Draupadi always eats last—after everyone is fed.

Uncooked jungle berries become a powerful metaphor in both epics, especially in the folk retellings. In regional retellings of the *Ramayana*, we hear how the old tribal lady Shabari bites into berries (ber) and gives the sweetest berry to Ram. This annoys Lakshman who sees the 'second-hand' food as an insult to Ram. But Ram accepts the berry as it is given with love. He does not see the offering as 'second-hand'. This idea of making food 'second-hand' or 'jootha' is a very important theme in India. Food thus contaminated is seen as impure and unfit for a sacred offering. Pure food is virginal—'first-hand'. By accepting the berry offered by Shabari, Ram challenges the notions of purity—of food, women, men, and the orthodox society in general.

In regional retellings of the *Mahabharata*, the purple Indian gooseberry (jambul) plays an important role. Draupadi plucks a jambul, angering a sage who was looking forward to eating it. He threatens to curse Draupadi's husbands unless Draupadi is able to reattach the fruit to the plant. He tells her that she can do it if she reveals the deepest darkest secret in her heart. So Draupadi admits that, despite having five husbands, she is in love with Karna. Instantly, the fruit reattaches itself to the plant. And we are told that the fruit will stain the mouths of all those who have secrets in their hearts purple and such people must not judge Draupadi.

Thus, both the *Ramayana* and the *Mahabharata* use forest fruits (ber, jambul) and heroines to deal with complex issues of domestic life such as desire, fidelity, faithfulness and purity.

24

Both describe encounters with tribal communities

The tribal people of the forest live on hunting and gathering, prefer not to pursue agriculture and animal husbandry, reject the concept of private property, and try to blend in with the forest that is their home. In the *Ramayana*, they are called the Shabara people and in the *Mahabharata*, they are known as the Kirata. They are not like the rishis, who value the domestication of land and creation of culture as an expression of human potential.

In the *Valmiki Ramayana*, composed 2,000 years ago, Ram encounters the tribal woman Shabari. In this text, she is simply a student of Matanga rishi, who waits to see Ram. It is only in a much later version, the Odia *Dandi Ramayana* that she offers Ram mangoes and he picks one with toothmarks. This incident appears in the epic about 500 years ago, around the time Bhakti literature gained popularity. Only 300 years ago, in the Hindi version, we find for the first time the story of Shabari's berries. She is so happy to see Ram that she offers him berries, after tasting them herself. Lakshman is disgusted by her actions but Ram is more than happy for he knows she is doing it not to pollute the food (an elitist taboo) but to ensure that she offers him the sweetest berries.

In the *Mahabharata*, a tribal youth, Ekalavya, wants to learn archery from Drona. Drona refuses to teach him as he is not a Kshatriya. The boy teaches himself and becomes such an excellent archer that Arjuna grows insecure. Ekalavya claims that he still considers Drona his guru so Drona demands Ekalavya's thumb as his fee. Ekalavya gives Drona his thumb and, thus, is never ever able to hold the bow again. Later, in the forest during his exile, Arjuna fights a Kirata over a boar that both claim they have killed. The Kirata defeats Arjuna easily and reprimands him for being an entitled prince. Arjuna recognizes the Kirata as Shiva.

Thus, both stories refer to the tribal people of India who are outside the four-fold community (chatur-varna) system of mainstream Vedic society. We notice that they are seen as unrefined but dignified. In both stories, their innocence comes through— an innocence that is celebrated by Ram and taken advantage of by Drona. Krishna even marries a 'bear' woman, suggesting the inclusion of tribal communities into the mainstream.

25

Both feature interactions with sages in the forest

Rishis or sages were people who travelled to unchartered lands, carrying the Vedic way with them. They usually followed the path (marga) created by deer (mriga), as it led to waterbodies, critical for the survival of a settlement. Rishis were associated with the ritual of yagna. The water of the tirtha and fire of the yagna are critical for establishing human settlements; without water and fire, there cannot be a village.

Rajanyas, or warriors, who were proficient with the bow and arrow, followed the rishis. They then conducted the ashwamedha ritual, and used their horses to establish themselves as kings and claim the surrounding territory. This is probably the reason why both epics refer to kings being sent to the forest, where they repeatedly encounter sages, who perform yagnas, close to waterbodies.

What do you do in the forest? If you are a warrior, you spend your time hunting deer, for meat, skin and bones, and defending yourself against hostile tribes, and demons. But in the *Ramayana* and the *Mahabharata*, great value is placed on meeting sages and visiting holy places. So, across India, there are many sacred spots such as caves, ponds and waterfalls, described as places once visited by either Ram or the Pandavas.

In the *Ramayana*, Ram encounters many sages such as

Sharabhanga, Sutikshna and Agastya. The sages invite Ram to stay with them but he politely declines, as he does not want to cause them distress by his hunting habit. The names of some of the sages, such as Salilahara (one-who-eats-water) and Vayubhakshana (one-who-eats-air), suggest they are ascetics who indulge in extreme fasting.

In the *Mahabharata* too, the Pandavas encounter many sages, including Vrihadashwa, who tells them the story of Nala and Damayanti; Markandeya, who tells them the story of Ram (Ramopakhyan) and that of Savitri and Satyavan; and finally, Pulatsya and Dhaumya, who tell them to visit various pilgrim sites (tirtha).

In the *Ramayana*, Ram first stays in Chitrakuta, then moves via the Dandaka forest to Panchavati, and after Sita's abduction, journeys via Kishkinda towards the southern coast. This shows a southward orientation of the *Ramayana*. It must be kept in mind that the analysis of the oldest retelling of the *Ramayana*, the *Valmiki Ramayana*, makes one wonder if the epic is familiar with the southern half of India, or for that matter, even the Gangetic plain, and if the word 'samudra' actually refers to a wide river or a confluence of rivers. This is highly controversial, as according to popular understanding, Ram did travel to the southern tip of India, and even established the temple of Rameswaram at the seashore. In Sri Lanka, there are spots identified with Sita's sojourn in the Lanka of the epic, although cynics argue that these are local inventions to boost the tourist trade of Hindus from India.

In the *Mahabharata*, the Pandavas keep moving between the Kamyaka and Dvaita forests, staying four times in Kamyaka and three times in Dvaita. The orientation is northwards, with special attention given to the Himalayas. The Badari-nath and Kedarnath temples in Uttarakhand are also linked to Pandava visits. We are told that the rainbows from the top of the Himalayan ranges take one towards swarga, the abode of Indra and other gods. But guided by sages, they visit pilgrim spots across the rest of the subcontinent, including Kashi, in the Gangetic plains; Ujjain in central India, referred to in the epic as Mahakala; Jwala-mukhi in Punjab, referred to in the epic as Vadava (tongue of fire); Gokarna in Karnataka; Mount Abu in Rajasthan; Prabhas in Gujarat; and Kanya-tirtha on the southernmost tip of India.

It must be kept in mind that in the epics, these are not the sacred spots we know today—associated with Shiva or Vishnu—but places where sages lived, mostly along the banks of rivers. This suggests that most activity during the time of the epics was concentrated in north India, around the Gangetic plains. Although Vedic civilization, thanks to the efforts of a few intrepid sages, had spread west to the Gulf of Kutch, and in the south right up to Tamil Nadu, much of the subcontinent, especially areas associated with tribal people, remained untouched by the Vedic way.

26

Both refer to rakshasas

The word 'evil' does not exist in Hindu mythology. All creatures are manifestations of the divine. But to stay alive, a living creature has to either feed on other living creatures, or compete with other living creatures. When this happens, the predator and the rival become our enemies. We hate them. We fear them. We call them villains, or worse, demons.

The rakshasas are forest-dwellers, sometimes called protectors (rakshaks) of the forest. This brings them in direct conflict with rishis who seek to domesticate the earth and the mind to create culture (sanskriti) out of nature (prakriti). To the rishi, the rakshasa is a demon who needs to be tamed as he has not outgrown the law of the jungle—which says that might is right. Hence, there is always a conflict between the rakshasas and rishis, which forms the backdrop of both the *Ramayana* and the *Mahabharata*.

In the *Ramayana*, Ram is specifically called to protect the rishis from attacks by the rakshasas. Vishwamitra directs him to kill Tataka and her companions, Subahu and Marich. Later, Ram kills Khar and Dushan. Finally, Ram fights and defeats Ravana, the king of the rakshasas, his allies, Kumbhakarna and Mahiravana, and his army.

In the *Mahabharata*, the Pandavas encounter many rakshasas.

When they first take refuge in the forest after their palace is set aflame, they encounter Jata, Baka and Hidimba. Bhima kills all of them, to the delight of the villagers who live on the edge of the forest. In fact, he so impresses the rakshasas that Hidimiba's sister, Hidimbi, marries him and they have a child together, called Ghatotkacha. When the Pandavas enter the forest as exiles, they encounter Kirimira, another rakshasa, who fights and is killed by Bhima.

It is interesting to note that in the *Mahabharata*, the rakshasas are called asuras. And it is common to use the two words interchangeably. In Hindu mythology, there are different kinds of demons. There are the asuras who fight the devas. There are rakshasas who fight the rishis. The deva-asura conflict is vertical, as devas live in the sky; and the rakshasa-rishi conflict is horizontal, as both live on earth. But rakshasas live in harmony with the forest, while rishis seek to tame forests and cultivate them into fields.

In the *Ramayana*, the rakshasas come across as highly civilized. Their leader, Ravana, is not entirely a rakshasa—his father is a rishi called Vishrava. Vishrava has another son, by a yaksha woman, called Kubera, who builds the golden city of Lanka. Ravana overpowers Kubera to become the king of Lanka. So the rakshasas we encounter in the *Ramayana* are a mix of rakshasas and rishis—the wild and the domestic.

In the *Ramayana*, Vishwamitra explicitly asks Ram to protect the rishis from attacks by the rakshasas. It may be inferred that rakshasas were non-Vedic people, who saw rishis as intruders and invaders. This hypothesis is plausible because in later times, in and around Tamil Nadu especially, kings would send Brahmins to create new villages (brahmadeya villages)—in tandem with how rishis are described as creating the earliest settlements in Vedic times. They would establish a temple, and a whole new community would emerge around it—a community that paid taxes to the king in exchange for the security wealth generated.

In the *Mahabharata*, when the forest of Khandava is set on fire, an asura called Maya seeks the protection of the Pandavas and offers to build them a great city. Is he a rakshasa or someone else? We are not sure. During the war, the rakshasas fight on both sides. Ghatotkacha, the son of Bhima, fights for the Pandavas while Alambusha, another rakshasa, fights for the Kauravas.

The rishis gave great value to the yagna, a ritual that involves exchange—giving and getting (not giving and taking). Exchange is a human trait. Animals do not exchange, they cannot exchange, except a few species of bats and chimpanzees (but only with familiar members of their own species). Human culture is based on, and expands with, exchange. Or we can say that the rishis sought to domesticate the wild earth and the wild human mind. This naturally brought them in conflict with those who lived in the forest, who preferred to take, rather than exchange. The forest-dwellers followed the law of the jungle and resisted civilization, which brings with it the destruction of nature.

27

Both refer to gandharvas and apsaras

Gandharvas are creatures associated with fragrance (gandha, in Sanskrit). They are musicians often found in the company of apsaras. However, in the epics *Ramayana* and *Mahabharata*, they are forest creatures that Ram and the Pandavas encounter during their exile.

In the *Ramayana*, a demon called Viradha tries to abduct Sita. He cannot be killed by weapons. So, when Ram and Lakshman catch him, they break his bones and bury him alive. As he dies, a gandharva emerges from the demonic body and identifies himself as Tumburu. He thanks Ram for rescuing him. Later, after Sita is abducted by Ravana, another such demon called Kabandha, whose head has merged with his torso, catches hold of Ram and Lakshman and tries to eat them. When Kabandha is killed, a gandharva emerges from the demon's body and identifies himself as Vishwavasu, thanking Ram for rescuing him. Thus, gandharvas appear in the *Ramayana*, hidden in the body of monsters, and are liberated when Ram kills these monsters.

In the *Mahabharata* too, the gandharvas are forest-dwellers. A gandharva called Chitrasena attacks and kills Satyavati's son who shares the same name. Arjuna encounters and defeats a gandharva called Angaraparna, who in gratitude, gives Arjuna horses and chariots, and advises him to take Dhaumya as his family priest. Another gandharva called Chitraratha teaches Arjuna to dance and sing when Arjuna visits swarga, the paradise of Indra. Yet another attacks and takes Duryodhana hostage, when the Kauravas enter the forest to gloat about the Pandavas' suffering during exile. Arjuna has to intervene and save an embarrassed Duryodhana.

Apsaras are creatures associated with water (apsa, in Sanskrit). They are nymphs, embodiments of enchantment, and companions of the love-god Kama. They dance in the abode of the gods, and distract sages from their meditation. They play minor but pivotal roles in the *Ramayana* and the *Mahabharata*.

In the *Ramayana*, the sight of an apsara called Urvashi so excites the celibate sage Vibhandaka that he loses control over his senses and spills semen on the grass that is consumed by a female deer who eventually gives birth to Shringa rishi. This Shringa rishi or Rishyashringa-muni performs the yagna that enables Dasharatha to become the father of four sons. The other significant apsara in the *Ramayana* is Rambha, who Ravana forces himself upon. She curses the rakshasa-king that should he ever force himself on another woman, his head will split into a thousand pieces. This is why Ravana restrains himself and does not force himself on Sita.

In the *Mahabharata*, Pururava, an ancestor of the Pandavas, falls in love with Urvashi and loses his mind when she leaves for swarga without him. Later in the epic, when Arjuna visits swarga to meet his father, Indra, he encounters Urvashi. She wants to lie with him but he refuses, arguing that since she was married to his ancestor, it would be inappropriate for him to touch her. Urvashi gets angry at this logic, as the rules for celestial beings are different from the rules for ordinary mortals. She curses Arjuna that since he rejected her, he is not fit to be a man. He will lose his genitals and become a eunuch. Indra uses his power to restrict the curse for a year. Thus, Arjuna lives out his curse as a eunuch-dancer, called Brihanalla, in the court of Virata in the final year of his exile.

In the Puranas, the gandharvas and apsaras accompany Kama, the love-god, on his adventures to enchant and seduce sages to give up their celibate lives and become worldly people. In the *Ramayana* and the *Mahabharata*, the gandharvas are more wild forest creatures than musicians, but the apsaras do fulfil their roles as divine damsels. They embody the spirit of the forest, untamed by culture.

28

Both refer to snake-people

Nagas or the snake-people play a key role in Hindu, Buddhist and Jain scriptures. Who were they? Were they non-Vedic agricultural people who worshipped snakes and were overthrown or driven into forests by the Aryas? We can only speculate. In the Puranas, they live under the earth, in the fabulous world known as Rasa-tala, located in the city of Bhoga-vati, ruled by Vasuki. They are known for their shape-shifting nature, as well as the gems they possess which can cure all ailments. They play a key role in both the *Ramayana* and the *Mahabharata*.

In a later retelling of the *Ramayana*, Ravana's son, Indrajit, also known as Meghanad, is married to Sulochana, a naga princess, and so, he has many magical weapons gifted to him by the serpents. Using this naga-astra, he is able to capture Hanuman, who wreaks havoc in Ravana's garden. Armed with the knowledge of naga-astra he is able to bind Ram and Lakshman in battle, until Garuda comes to their rescue from Vaikuntha. When Lakshman finally kills Indrajit, his head reaches Lanka but his body remains in the battlefield. The rakshasas are too terrified to go and fetch the corpse, so his widow, Sulochana, ventures forth on her own, earning the admiration of Ram for her courage. In the Assamese retelling of *Ramayana*, in the final chapter, after Sita refuses to return to Ayodhya and descends into the earth, she takes up residence in Rasa-tala and gets the serpents to abduct her sons— Luv and Kush—whom she misses very much. This leads to a war between the nagas and Ram and eventually Sita lets her sons return to Ayodhya and promises to visit Ram secretly.

In the *Mahabharata*, the Pandavas and Krishna are related to the nagas. When the Kauravas attempt to kill Bhima by poisoning and throwing him into the river, the nagas rescue him and give him an antidote. Bhima marries a naga princess and from that union is born a son who participates in the great war of the *Mahabharata*. Arjuna too marries the naga princess Ulupi and from their union is born Aravan, who also participates in the war. When the Pandavas burn the Khandava forest, they effectively destroy the home of the nagas, many of whom are killed. One of the survivors, Ashwasena, enters the quiver of Karna, and takes the form of an arrow, with which Karna shoots Arjuna. Arjuna is rescued, as Krishna causes his chariot to sink in the ground and the arrow strikes Arjuna's crown instead. Ashwasena once again approaches Karna, but Karna refuses to shoot the same arrow twice. Another survivor, Takshaka, ends up killing Parikshit, the grandson of Arjuna. Parikshit's son, Janamejaya, conducts a sacrifice to kill all the serpents but is stopped by the half-naga, half-human Astika who asks him to listen to the story of the *Mahabharata* to understand the futility of vengeance.

In Vaishnava literature, whenever Vishnu descends on earth, he is accompanied by the cosmic serpent Adi-Sesha who serves as Vishnu's throne. When Vishnu is Ram, Adi-Sesha is Lakshman; when Vishnu is Krishna, Adi-Sesha is Balarama.

Some scholars are of the opinion that the antecedent to snake worship is much older in India, an alternative way of thinking which gradually mingled with Vedic thought. It was the religion of the tribal people who were gradually displaced by agricultural communities. However, they were never wiped out. They demanded assimilation. Hence, the serpent sheltering the sage, or god, is a common motif not just in Hindu temples, but also in Buddhist and Jain shrines. The serpents were associated with rain and fertility, approached for good harvest and children. Today, we see them as an essential constituent of Hindu mythology. However, at one time, they were probably a separate tributary, often in conflict with Vedic ideas.

29

Both refer to alternate realities

A world with a good king is utopia and a world with a bad king is dystopia. In both the *Ramayana* and the *Mahabharata*, we are told that the rule of Ram and Yudhishthira will create utopia. We are also introduced to dystopian realities. In utopia, the king energizes his people to take care of the weak. In dystopia, the king drains his people of energy and makes them insecure, so that they let themselves be dominated and dominate others in return.

And so, in the *Ramayana* we encounter the kingdom of Kishkinda, which Vali and Sugriva are supposed to share; but following a misunderstanding, Vali behaves like an alpha male and drives Sugriva away, claiming all the trees and females of the monkey troop for himself. Later, in Lanka, Ram encounters a king who is willing to let his brother (Kumbhakarna), son (Indrajit) and subjects die rather than make peace.

In the *Mahabharata*, the kingdom of Virata is dystopia. Here, the Pandavas have to experience what it means to be a servant: Yudhishthira is the game-companion of the king, Bhima is a cook, Arjuna is a stable keeper, Nakula and Sahadeva work in the cattle sheds and horse stables, and Draupadi is the queen's hairdresser. They come face-to-face with the abuse domestic servants have to endure. Yudhishthira is slapped by the king for being too honest.

Arjuna is made fun of for being transgender. Draupadi is sexually harassed by the king's brother-in-law, Kichaka.

These dystopian realities are meant to show us why we need kings to uphold dharma. Ram and Yudhishthira are constantly reminded why the weak need protection from the strong. We also learn that a king is not one who makes people dependent on him, but rather one who makes others, and himself, dependable.

V

War

In which we discuss the negotiations and preparations before war, as well as the glamour and moral dilemmas associated with war

30

Both refer to the importance of allies and negotiations

Chanakya in his *Artha-shastra* states that a king needs allies and an army to manage his enemies. Both the *Ramayana* and the *Mahabharata* elaborate on how kings need to create allies if they hope to fight and get back what belongs to them.

In the *Ramayana*, when Ram and Lakshman learn that Sita has been abducted by the demon-king Ravana, they look for allies to help them find and rescue Sita. And this leads them to an encounter with the monkey kingdom where they make a number of allies. Ram's allies are animals—vultures, bears, monkeys and squirrels. In his presence, animals are able to reverse the law of jungle and help humans. The vultures find out where Sita has been taken, the bears and squirrels help in building the bridge to Lanka, and the monkeys fight the rakshasas of Lanka and help liberate Sita.

In the *Mahabharata*, the Pandavas are supported by the Panchalas, the father and the brothers of Draupadi. Their uncles, the Yadavas and the Madras, end up fighting for the Kaurava side; the Yadavas because Krishna tells the two sides to choose between him and his fully-equipped army, the Madras because their king mistakenly assumes that those feeding his army en route are Pandavas and promises to lead them to victory.

Balarama refuses to fight for either side. Rukmi, Krishna's brother-in-law, is not accepted by either side. The sons of Arjuna and Bhima fight for the Pandavas. The division is mostly based on relationships and obligations, and not on dharma. Bhishma, Drona and Karna fight for the Kauravas not because they are upholding dharma, but because they value loyalty over everything else.

Peace is always preferable to war. In both the *Ramayana* and the *Mahabharata* there are attempts to make peace, with emissaries being sent from both sides to negotiate and avoid war.

In the *Ramayana*, Vali's son, Angada, is sent to declare war or make peace with Ravana. Though young in age, Angada proves his strength before Ravana by challenging the rakshasas to move his feet, which are planted firmly to the ground. They fail. Angada speaks of Ram's glory and advises Ravana to do the right thing and return Ram's wife. Ravana refuses, despite the entreaties of his entire family, including his father, mother and wife. Finally, war is declared. And the monkey army, armed with sticks and stones, attacks the fully-armed rakshasa army of Ravana.

In the *Mahabharata*, two messengers are sent from the Pandava side and two from the Kaurava side to make peace and compromise. Satyaki tells the Pandavas to send an envoy only after ensuring they have strength on their side. While gathering allies, the Pandavas discover that the Kauravas have already managed to take many kings to their side. Drupada's envoy, who asks that the Pandava land be returned, is sent back humiliated. Sanjaya tells the Pandavas not to return. Uluka insults the Pandavas and tells them not to ask for what is not theirs. Krishna tries to broker peace, attempts a compromise, but fails. Even the offer to give the Pandavas just five villages is rejected by Duryodhana who does not want to part with even a needlepoint of land. Krishna then tries to divide the Kauravas by wooing Karna to the Pandava side. All these negotiations form an entire chapter—the 'Udyoga Parva'—before the war.

31

Both refer to fabulous weapons

In the *Ramayana*, whenever Sita is thirsty, Ram shoots an arrow into the ground and outpours a spring. In the *Mahabharata*, Arjuna does the same—whether it is to quench the thirst of his horses, or to quench the thirst of the dying Bhishma. Thus, in both epics, arrows are not just arrows—they are missiles.

We are told that in ancient times, rishis could turn a simple arrow into a missile with the power of mantra. Through mantras, they could inject into an arrow, the power of a god. Thus, one could create Agni-astra, using the power of the fire-god, Vayu-astra, using the power of the wind-god, Varuna-astra, using the power of the water-god, and Naga-astra, using the power of the serpent-god. While ordinary weapons could only kill one person, a mantra-charged astra could kill many.

In the *Ramayana*, Ram raises such an astra against Varuna, the God of the sea, and Varuna begs him to stop. He tells Ram to build a bridge over him instead of asking him to part the water and make a passage. Ram agrees, but knows that an arrow once mounted has to be released, and so he releases it northwards and the place struck by it turns into what we now know as the Thar Desert. Eventually, it is only by using the Brahma-astra that Ram is able to kill Ravana, for the rakshasa-king is too powerful.

In the *Mahabharata*, Arjuna and Karna shoot such terrible missiles at each other that they scorch the skies and the earth. In the final chapter, an angry Ashwathama releases the Brahma-astra and Arjuna releases a missile to counter it. Vyasa begs the two of them to pull it back and warns that if they strike each other, nature will be destroyed forever. Some people believe that the description of the after-effects of the missile strike in the epic indicates that ancient Indians had predicted the aftermath of nuclear warfare. Arjuna is able to pull back his arrow but not Ashwathama, who directs his arrow towards the unborn child in Abhimanyu's wife Uttara's womb. Krishna saves the child, but curses Ashwathama that he will live a miserable life with unhealing, festering, pus-oozing wounds.

We are told that these arrows are used to build roofs over yagna-shalas and to build bridges over rivers.

In the *Ramayana*, when Hanuman is flying back, carrying the Dronagiri mountain of herbs, he is shot down by Bharat as he is flying over Ayodhya. Hanuman relates his tale to Bharat and tells him of the plight of Ram and Lakshman. To help him reach Lanka on time, Bharat shoots a powerful arrow that carries Hanuman, with the mountain in hand.

In the *Mahabharata*, Bhishma uses arrows to block the flow of River Ganga and Arjuna uses arrows to create a bridge that enables Airavata, Indra's elephant, to descend from the sky to the earth, for the pleasure of his mother.

While Ram has the power to use these astras, he hesitates to use them. By contrast, the heroes of the *Mahabharata* are eager to use these astras. Perhaps the poets wanted to convey that wise men don't show their strength, while strong men lacking wisdom do.

32

Both deal with flying saucers

Many Hindus believe that ancient Indians had access to aeroplanes, or flying machines, known as vimana. Even Jain scriptures refer to the flying palaces or vimana of celestial beings, that many have taken to mean flying saucers.

Vimana means that which 'measures out'—or that which stretches our mind. In architecture, it alludes to the grand pyramidal tower above the room where the deity is enshrined in a temple. It refers to the chariot of the gods. In Vedic times, mantras were chanted to invoke and invite the gods for a meal; they would come on their flying chariots, which in Puranic times were visualized as grand temples with towers, and many floors and pillars. Are these flying chariots referring to the psychological state that elevates us towards divine potential, or are they real things—objects created by ancient scientists and architects?

There is no archaeological evidence and the current knowledge of aeronautics indicates that the structures described could not possibly have been airborne. Across the world, there are many gigantic pyramidal structures, such as the pyramids of Giza, Egypt, leading to speculations that ancient people, in collaboration with aliens, built these structures that gave them the power of flight. Many argue that ancient Vedic wisdom enabled rishis to acquire the power (siddhi) of telekinesis which allowed them to travel in flying chariots. Many are offended if this is classified as wishful thinking or a fantasy to prop up a sense of inadequacy. But it must be kept in mind that the force with which some people argue about the existence of aeroplanes in India's ancient history is matched with equal force by the same people who insist there was no homosexuality in ancient India.

That being said, both the *Ramayana* and the *Mahabharata* do contain references to flying chariots.

The *Ramayana* is famous for the pushpak-vimana of Ravana. It was built by Kubera, the yaksha-king, who used it to travel around the world. It was usurped by Ravana, who used it to terrorize the world. Ravana brings Sita to Lanka, over the sea, on this chariot. Later, Ram returns to Ayodhya on this chariot. The vimana is sometimes imagined as being pulled by birds, just as regular chariots are pulled by horses.

In the *Mahabharata*, the flying chariot is in the background. One wonders where Krishna is when the Pandavas enter the gambling hall of the Kauravas. We are told, in the Puranas, that he is busy fighting the friends of Shishupala. Krishna beheads

Shishupala at Indraprastha during Yudhishthira's coronation. In retaliation, Shishupala's friend, Shalva, attacks Krishna's city of Dwarka with his flying vimana. While Krishna is busy fighting Shalva, the Pandavas gamble away their kingdom.

33

Both refer to ends justifying the means

In warrior communities known for their heroism and valour in the battlefield, such as the Rajputs, a great warrior always faces his enemy from the front. Yet, in the *Ramayana* Ram kills the monkey-king Vali by shooting him while he is busy duelling his brother, Sugriva. And in the *Mahabharata*, Krishna encourages Arjuna to kill Karna while he is busy pulling out the wheel of his chariot that is stuck in mud. Is this right or wrong?

The desire to judge comes from Abrahamic mythologies (Judaism, Christianity and Islam), where God makes the rules and acts as a judge. But in Hinduism, God is not a judge. The two epics are based on karma, dharma and atma.

In dharma, rules exist only to enable the mighty to take care of the meek. Rules that favour the mighty are no rules at all. Hence, rules that favour Vali over Sugriva in the *Ramayana* and the Kauravas over the Pandavas in the *Mahabharata* are disregarded by Ram and Krishna.

In karma, fortune in the present is determined by the actions of past lifetimes. This makes events in the *Mahabharata* a reaction to the events in the *Ramayana*. In the *Ramayana*, Ram favours Surya's son (Sugriva) over Indra's son (Vali) and so, in the *Mahabharata*, Vishnu as Krishna is obliged to favour Indra's son (Arjuna) over Surya's son (Karna)—so that the account book of action and reaction is balanced.

Aham is a function of insecurity and so makes the mighty, despite having wealth and power, exploit and dominate the meek. In the *Ramayana*, Vali is driven by aham when he refuses to share the kingdom with Sugriva, as per their father's wishes. In the *Mahabharata*, Karna is driven by aham when he values the role of the chariot-riding archer (rathi) over the chariot-driver (sarathi). The Pandavas are also driven by aham when they constantly mock Karna as a charioteer's son (suta-putra), not realizing that Karna is actually their elder brother. Krishna embodies atma and has no problem being seen as a cowherd (gopala) or a charioteer. He can see beyond social status, at the soul within. To rise above petty social hierarchy is atma-gyan.

34

Both are ambiguous about loyalty

Is loyalty good or bad? Common wisdom tells us that loyalty is a virtue, a sign of integrity. However, in the *Ramayana* and the *Mahabharata*, the loyal are punished and the traitors rewarded. In the *Ramayana*, the loyal Kumbhakarna is killed while the traitor Vibhishana is made king of the world. In the *Mahabharata*, the loyal Bhishma, Drona, Karna, Shalya and Vikarna are killed, while the traitor Yuyutsu is rewarded.

This perplexes scholars with a linear (Western) view of the world, but not those who are able to appreciate a cyclical (Indian) view of the world; for as we have seen, Hindu mythology does not bother with binaries like right/wrong, good/bad, and loyal/traitor. It deals with the binary of aham/atma, limited/limitless, fear/wisdom, and dependent/dependable. In other words, it functions on a different axis.

The question to be asked is: What *is* loyalty? Why do we valorize it? In nature, there is no loyalty. Animals are hardwired to be part of a pack or a herd or a hive, as it increases their chances of survival. Humans are loyal for two reasons—it increases their chances of survival, or it nourishes their self-image. This is aham at work. We seek loyalty as it makes us feel secure. This is also aham at work. The atma is not insecure or hungry, and so, it neither gives loyalty nor expects loyalty.

Loyalty reveals dependence. The purpose of atma-gyan is to move away from dependence and be independent so that one can eventually be dependable. Brahma and his children are dependent, seeking and providing loyalty, hence, unworthy of worship. Shiva is independent, neither seeking nor providing loyalty, hence, worshipped as a hermit. Vishnu is dependable, does not need loyalty, does not provide loyalty, but is able to appreciate the insecurities that make humans value loyalty.

In the *Ramayana*, Ravana's brothers make choices. Vibhishana opposes Ravana and sides with Ram. Kumbhakarna also opposes Ravana, but fights by his side. In supporting Ravana, Kumbhakarna provides nourishment to Ravana's insecurities and further fuels his aham. Thus, he contributes to adharma. He cannot handle being a traitor, even though disloyalty here would be a function of wider wisdom.

In the *Mahabharata*, Bhishma is loyal, as he cares more for the name of the Kuru clan than dharma; Drona is loyal, as he cares more for royal power than dharma; Karna is loyal because he is indebted to Duryodhana and values that more than dharma; Shalya is loyal because he is tricked into promising his army to Duryodhana; Vikarna is loyal, despite opposing Duryodhana, because Duryodhana is a brother; Dusshasana is loyal because he refuses to think, unlike Vikarna. Yuyutsu, however, changes sides. He chooses dharma over loyalty. He is admired not for opposing the Kauravas but for upholding dharma.

For whom do you fight is the question to ask. The loyal person serves the other to nourish his aham. The one who follows dharma knows that he only serves atma—not Ram or Krishna, but the larger idea of humanity, where the mighty take care of the meek.

35

Both refer to Shudra-killing

In the early verses of the *Rig Veda*, we see that the world is divided into rishis (keepers of Vedic lore) and rajanyas (warriors and cattle-herders). Later, we see the rise of four categories (chatur-varna) of people who carry the lore of Brahmanas (Brahmins), people who control kshetra (Kshatriyas), the product-makers and traders (Vaishya), and the service-providers (Shudra). Aham creates hierarchy and assumes Brahmins are superior to Shudras, while atma dissolves hierarchy by acknowledging the four varnas as simply four categories to make sense of diverse vocations that sustain the society. Beyond this four-fold system existed the forest tribes (Nishadha) and beyond them, the barbarians (Mlechha).

In the *Ramayana* and the *Mahabharata*, there are many encounters with forest tribes described as rakshasa, asura, gandharva, yaksha, kapi or vanara, and kirata. Some are friendly, some hostile. There is also a lot of tension between the varnas—the Brahmins, the Kshatriyas and the Shudras. The Vaishyas are by and large absent from the epics. They play major roles in the Jatakas.

Varna is sometimes translated as 'caste', a term introduced by the Portuguese to explain the clans they found in India—clans that followed a particular vocation and isolated themselves from other jatis by not sharing food (roti) and daughters (beti). A more appropriate word for caste is 'jati'.

In India, there are thousands of jatis—some exist across India, while others are found regionally. The Brahmins classified these jatis into a four-tier system such that they were on top, and the local landowners and kings were placed in the second tier. They did not care for the rest. The most affected by this system were those involved in vocations that were considered 'impure'—those whose work involved working with garbage, sewage, dead bodies, leather, bones and flesh. They were considered 'untouchables' and denied access to the village well. This group of people are missing from the two epics, but there are many stories that speak of the importance of caste, and the significance of following one's vocation, no matter what.

In the *Ramayana*, Ram calls the boatman, Guha, his brother for ferrying him across the Ganga. Later, upon his return to Ayodhya, he beheads Shambuka for choosing to be a hermit rather than fulfilling his caste duties. Shambuka's action, we are told, disrupts the natural order, as indicated by the death of a Brahmin child before his father. Here, Ram is enforcing varna dharma in his role as a king to maintain social order. What was Shambuka's profession? We don't know, but he is often identified as a Shudra.

In the *Mahabharata*, Karna does not want to follow his foster father's profession. He wants to be an archer. He is constantly insulted by Pandavas for not following his father's profession. In the war, he is killed not when he is holding the bow but while he is changing the wheel of his chariot. In other words, he is put in his place.

The Pandavas feel they are superior because they are born in a family of Kshatriyas. But in the final year of their exile, all Pandavas have to live as servants in the palace of Virata, and suffer humiliation at the hands of the royal family. Yudhishthira is companion to the king and is slapped once. Bhima is a cook and has to feed others before he can eat himself. Arjuna, who loves to enchant women, has to live like a cross-dressing eunuch, teaching dance to the princess. Nakula and Sahadeva work in the horse stables and cowsheds. Draupadi is hairdresser to the queen and is sexually harassed by the queen's brother, Kichaka. Thus, the future kings are taught to respect the service-providers.

Krishna has no problems projecting himself as a cowherd and charioteer, rather than a king, reminding us all that to see oneself as superior to others is to indulge the aham and move away from the atma.

36

Both refer to Brahmin-killing

In Hinduism, Brahmin-killing or brahma-hatya is the worst of crimes. That being said, Brahmin-killing is a consistent theme in the two epics as well as in the later Puranas, where Ram kills Ravana, Krishna enables the killing of Drona, Shiva beheads Brahma and Daksha, and is even called Kapalika—he who holds a Brahmin's skull in his hand. This makes Brahmin-killing a deliberately recurring Puranic theme that seeks to express and communicate a cultural thought. So much for the Brahminical hegemony of Hindu scriptures!

In the Upanishads, 'brahman' (no vowel stressed) means an 'expanding mind'; whereas 'brAhmaN' (first vowel stressed and last consonant stressed) refers to ritual manuals, as well as their caretakers—also known as Brahmins. There is also 'brahmA' (second vowel stressed) who is the 'creator' and 'father of all living things' in Puranic mythology.

A Brahmin was supposed to transmit knowledge of Brahmanas through ritual. Knowledge of Brahmanas expands the mind so that we are able to overpower the law of the jungle (matsya-nyaya), stop indulging aham, appreciate the atma and follow dharma. However, in the two epics, Brahmins are less interested in expanding the mind and following dharma, and more interested in indulging aham.

Ravana is the son of Vaishrava and Drona is the son of Bharadvaja. Both Vaishrava and Bharadvaja are well-versed in the Vedas. Ravana is an expert in Vedic astrology (jyotisha-shastra) and geomancy (vastu-shastra), but he chooses to be a warrior, and later a king, usurping his brother Kubera's kingdom and declaring himself the king of Lanka. Drona, on the other hand, learns the Vedas from his father, and later, Vedic martial arts (dhanur-vidya) from Parashurama. Drona expressly disobeys Parashurama who had forbidden him from teaching Kshatriyas when he served as a tutor to the Kuru princes. Drona also functions as a warrior, a general to the Kaurava army, and ensures that his son, Ashwathama, becomes king. Instead of following their caste vocation, these men indulge their aham and become ambitious.

Insecurity fuels Ravana's and Drona's quest for wealth and power. Ravana is willing to let his brothers and sons die, and his kingdom burn, than allow Sita to return to her husband. Drona has no problem getting his students to attack Drupada's kingdom in the name of dakshina so as to extract his revenge. Drona does not see anything wrong in cutting Ekalavya's thumb to ensure the supremacy of Arjuna. Drona is so attached to his son that he is unable to fight when he hears rumours that Ashwathama may be dead. In the Puranas, Brahma lusts after his own creation, and Daksha sees Shiva as 'impure'. Such behaviour is unacceptable and fuels adharma in the world—the loss of humanity. And so, God in the form of Ram and Krishna, and Shiva in the Puranas, beheads the Brahmin just as he beheaded the Shudra for not following the caste duties.

Varna dharma made economic sense in old agrarian feudal economies to secure the vocation of communities over generations. However, it does not make sense in industrial and post-industrial economies. Today, greater value is placed on individual vocation and ambition. We can be boatmen, hermits, charioteers, cowherds, warriors—whatever we want to be, and that is okay, provided we do not use our vocation to indulge aham, and follow adharma.

VI

Aftermath

In which we recognize how the stories are not about triumph, but about reflection—about the forest and the animal nature of humanity.

37

Both have two endings

How does the *Ramayana* end? With the coronation of Ram, or with the death of Ram? How does the *Mahabharata* end? With the coronation of Yudhishthira, or with his ascent to paradise? Both the *Ramayana* and the *Mahabharata* have two endings— one that deals with triumph over a villain, and the other which is more contemplative, pondering over the meaning of our existence. The first ending is heroic, grand and celebratory; the second ending is tragic, meditative and melancholy. The first ending is material victory, or vijaya; the second ending is spiritual victory, or jaya.

If we view the epics as tales about the destruction of villains, then the killing of Ravana and the Kauravas should mark the end of the respective epics. But clearly, they are not about victory over the villains alone. These are just episodes in a larger narrative. The *Ramayana* stretches from the birth of Ram to the death of Ram. The *Mahabharata* stretches from the birth of the Pandavas to the death of the Pandavas, and even includes tales of the birth and death of Krishna. Thus, the two epics are about entire lifetimes, a mixture of the highs and lows, and neither end in a heady climax that is solely positive or negative.

In traditional circles, the most auspicious (mangal) image is that of Ram on the throne with Sita by his side, Hanuman at his feet, and his brothers standing around him. This is Ram-patta-abhishek—the high, happy point of the epic. This, however, is followed by tragedy—street gossip about Sita, her rejection by Ram, the battle between Ram's forces and Luv and Kush over the royal sacrificial horse, the descent of Sita into the earth, and Ram willingly entering River Sarayu to give up his life.

In the *Mahabharata*, the most auspicious image is of Bhishma delivering a long speech about royal duties (raj dharma) to the Pandavas, as he lies on a bed of arrows. This is followed by the coronation of Yudhishthira, his horse-sacrifice, the ill treatment of Dhritarashtra by Bhima, the renunciation of the elders, and finally, the renunciation of the Pandavas, who seek to enter paradise (swarga) with their bodies, but all—except Yudhishthira—fail.

The two endings make us ponder over the purpose of life. Is it victory and achievements, like the first ending? Or is it an entire life, from birth to death, with sorrows and joys, defeats and triumphs, which gives our lives meaning? Victory does not necessarily mean happiness, as Ram and Krishna discover. Even in their victories, Ram is separated from Sita once more, while Gandhari curses Krishna, and Draupadi has to cope with the death of her sons. If the first ending deals with a focused objective, the second ending deals with a broader perspective. The audience is left to choose the ending and it is an outcome of his or her own emotional maturity.

Both speak of wailing widows

Valmiki was inspired to write the first poetry (adi kavya) based on Ram's life after he saw a hunter shoot an arrow that killed a male lovebird (krauncha), causing the female bird to wail over his dead body. Horrified, Valmiki cursed the hunter and the curse issued forth in the form of a verse. He uses this verse structure to write the entire *Ramayana* epic. The idea of a wailing widow (a bird in this case) recurs throughout the *Ramayana*. Tara wails for Vali who is killed by Ram's arrow. Mandodari wails for Ravana who is killed by Ram's arrow. Sita wails, as she is separated from Ram, first by Ravana and then by street gossip in Ayodhya.

In the *Mahabharata*, there is an entire section—the Stri Parva—which is devoted to the theme of widows in mourning. In this section, which draws our attention to the price of war, the entire battlefield is covered with corpses of valiant warriors, their limbs torn, heads smashed, and entrails ripped out. There is blood everywhere. The stench of rotting carcases fills the air. Wolves and vultures gather in the horizon, ready to swoop down and eat the human flesh. No one is around to claim the bodies as the women wail. Draupadi, who has gotten her vengeance, weeps for her sons, while an angry Gandhari curses Krishna.

Both speak of transmission of knowledge across generations

When we die, we leave behind our wealth, but take our knowledge with us. The only way to ensure the survival of our knowledge is to share it with others while we are still alive. This was especially true in ancient India when writing was not encouraged and oral transmission was preferred. Writing was introduced to India around 2,300 years ago, in the time of Mauryan kings who invented the Brahmi script. And so, both the *Ramayana* and the *Mahabharata* contain tales of transmission of knowledge, which means the older generation sharing its knowledge with the younger generation.

In the *Ramayana*, as Ravana is dying, Ram tells Lakshman that Ravana is a great scholar and he should receive knowledge from him before he dies. But Lakshman returns empty-handed. So, Ram goes and bows at Ravana's feet and begs him to share his knowledge. Ravana smiles and tells Ram that he did not share his knowledge with Lakshman because Lakshman stood at his head and demanded the knowledge with the arrogance of the triumphant, whereas Ram, although triumphant, sat at his feet and humbly asked for knowledge, as a student should. Ravana then shares his knowledge with Ram. This story comes from a regional version of the *Ramayana*.

In the *Mahabharata*, Krishna tells the Pandavas to sit next to the dying Bhishma and learn from him. Bhishma speaks for long hours on the various aspects of dharma. This constitutes two of the eighteen books of the epic—the Shanti and Anushasana parvas, the book of peace and the book of discipline. Only after sharing his knowledge does Bhishma die.

40

Both describe horse-sacrifice by the victorious

Horses are not native to most parts of India, but have regularly been imported from the northwestern regions. Yet, the horse and the horse-drawn chariot play a key role in the *Ramayana* and the *Mahabharata*. Ram leaves Ayodhya on a chariot drawn by horses. During his war with Ravana, Ram gets a horse-drawn chariot from Indra so that he can face Ravana on an equal footing. Krishna leaves Mathura in a chariot drawn by horses, and even abducts Rukmini on a chariot. The Pandavas and Kauravas fight on horse-drawn chariots. Neither Ram nor Krishna are visually depicted riding the horses—it is always the chariot. The act of horse riding demanded larger horses, which were probably bred after the epics were composed.

The sacrifice of the horse—ashwamedha yagna—was an

important Vedic ritual to establish the power of a king. In the yagna, a horse was let loose and allowed to freely travel for a year. The land it traversed unchallenged came under the rule of the king. If the horse was captured, then it was an act of war—a challenge to the king's authority. After the year was over, the horse was sacrificed. The violent ritual involved the chanting of rather obscene occult hymns that magically transmitted the horse's virility to the king.

In the *Ramayana*, Ram conducts the horse-sacrifice when he is crowned king of Ayodhya. In the *Mahabharata*, Yudhishthira conducts the horse-sacrifice when he is crowned king of Hastinapur. Shatrughna protects Ram's horse during its wanderings, while Arjuna protects Yudhishthira's horse during its wanderings.

The horse-sacrifice not only establishes the rule of the victorious king; it also reconciles many fractured relationships in both epics. In the *Ramayana*, it brings Ram closer to his sons, Luv and Kush. In the *Mahabharata*, it enables Yudhishtira to reconcile with estranged relatives, hostile neighbours and those who sided with the Kauravas.

The stories of Ram's and Yudhishithira's horse-sacrifices have inspired many independent epics. Ram's horse-sacrifice is part of a story called *Uttar Ramayana*—often seen as separate from the main *Ramayana*—which ends with the coronation of Ram. One Assamese retelling, the *Adbhuta Ramayana*, by Raghunatha Mahanta, speaks of how after Sita descends into the earth, she misses her children and so asks the serpent king, Vasuki, to kidnap her sons and bring them to her subterranean abode. Ram then sends Hanuman to bring his sons back. A war ensues, and finally, Sita agrees to return to earth secretly to spend time with Ram and their children.

In the fifteenth century, many kings encouraged the writing of *Jaimini Bharata*, a retelling of the *Mahabharata* that focused on the Ashwamedha Parva, which describes Yudhishtira's horse-sacrifice in terms of devotion to Krishna. Here, old enemies are reconciled, thanks to Krishna's intervention. Additionally, new kingdoms, such as the 'kingdom of women' ruled by Pramila, are encountered, and even the horse that is sacrificed goes to Vaikuntha.

The plots in Jaimini's *Mahabharata* are not found in Vyasa's *Mahabharata*. The story goes that one of Vyasa's students, Jaimini, had a few doubts and he sought his teacher, but Vyasa had already left on a pilgrimage. Markandeya advised Jaimini to talk to the four birds that had witnessed the event at Kurukshetra, as they could tell him what even Vyasa did not know.

An arrow from the battlefield had hit a bird flying overhead, causing her belly to open. Four eggs had fallen on the battlefield at Kurukshetra but had not broken as the earth was soft with blood. The bell of a war elephant had fallen on the four eggs and in its warmth four birds had been born. These birds had heard all the conversations and thoughts of those who had fought in the great Bharata war. Later, they had accompanied Yudhishthira's horse when it was roaming around the world and had witnessed its many adventures.

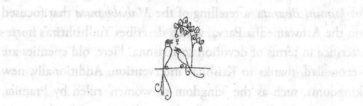

41

Both describe conflict between fathers and sons

During the horse-sacrifice, both the *Ramayana* and the *Mahabharata* tell us tales of a conflict between a father and a son.

In the *Ramayana*, the royal horse of Ram is captured by two boys, Luv and Kush, and they challenge the might of Ram's army. The boys defeat Ram's soldiers, as well as his brothers in battle. Even Hanuman is captured. Finally, Ram raises his bow and is about to shoot the arrows at them when Sita intervenes and informs Ram that the two boys are his own sons. By defeating Ram's army and capturing his horse, Ram's sons challenge his royal authority. The defeat of Ram by his sons, who have been raised by Sita, is seen as the triumph of Sita, who was wrongly cast out of Ayodhya following street gossip about her character.

A similar tale is found in the *Mahabharata*. During Yudhishthira's ashwamedha yagna, his horse is captured by Babruvahana, the king of Manipur. A fight follows between Arjuna and the king, in which Arjuna is defeated and killed. Babruvahana then learns from his horrified mother that Arjuna is his own father. As in the case of Luv and Kush, the father and the son have never met. Babruvahana further learns that the woman who taught him archery was Ulupi, one of Arjuna's wives, and this was her way of taking revenge on the man who had no recollection of her.

Ulupi blames Arjuna for the death of her son, Iravana, who had insisted on fighting in the Kuruskshetra war. So, she befriends Chitrangada, another wife of Arjuna, and trains Babruvahana in the art of war, well enough to defeat Arjuna—the great archer. But then, full of remorse, she decides to bring Arjuna back to life with the help of naga-mani, the sacred serpent jewel that can cure the injured. Arjuna comes back to life and is reunited with Babruvahana.

Both stories are unusual. Traditionally, in Indian stories, the son bows to the will of the father. This marks the triumph of the older generation over the younger generation. But here, the sons overpower their father, especially when they are not aware of his identity. Thus, the unknown or missing father faces the son's hostility. In both the stories, a single mother (Sita/Chitrangada-Ulupi) raises a son (Luv-Kush/Babruvahana), abandoned by the father (Ram/Arjuna).

42

Both have lives beyond the epic

In medieval folk ballads, at the intersection of Rajput folklore and Islam, we find tales of warriors and their valiant wives, who are often linked to characters from the *Ramayana* and the *Mahabharata*. Wishes unfulfilled in the Sanskrit epics serve as the seeds that germinate into characters and plots of the highly localized folk epics. There are many such folk epics, and versions of the folk epics—most of which are oral—making it difficult to find a 'standard' version. One can say that bards often mapped local stories to the *Ramayana* and the *Mahabharata* to make them seem grander and part of a larger cosmic design.

Characters from the *Ramayana* reappear in the Rajasthani ballad, *Pabuji*. Dadhal Rathore has a son, Baro, and a daughter, Pema. He falls in love with an apsara who gives him another son, the powerful Pabu (Lakshman). Baro inherits his father's land and cows, while Pabu, who inherits nothing, gets a magical flying horse from the goddess Deval (Sita) on the promise that he will always protect her cows. Jindhrav Khinchi (Ravana) desires the cows of Baro and Deval, but his daughter, Phulvati (Surpanakha), wants to marry Pabu. While the wedding rituals are underway, Jindhrav tries to steal the cows he so desires, but the goddess reminds Pabu of his promise. Forced to keep his word, Pabu leaves his own wedding midway to fight Jindhrav. In the fight that follows, Pabu is killed by a very reluctant Jindhrav. Phulvati who is half-married realizes that even though technically she may be Pabu's wife, Pabu is not her husband. Thus, Surpanakha's desire to marry Lakshman is fulfilled and so is Lakshman's desire to stay celibate. Baro's son, Rup, avenges Pabu's death by killing Jindhrav but renounces the throne to become a jogi—a student of the guru, Gorakhnath.

Characters from the *Mahabharata* reappear in the central Indian (Delhi, northeastern Madhya Pradesh, southwestern Uttar Pradesh) epic of Alha. The Pandavas wanted to die in battle like true Kshatriyas, and so are reborn as Alha (Yudhishthira), Udal (Bhima), Malkhan (Nakula) and Sulkhan (Sahadeva), who serve the king of Mahoba. These four guardians are often described as 'lower' caste, as their mothers are from the community of buffalo-herders. The guardians are trained in war by their father's friend, a Muslim warrior and a Sayyid from Kashi, called Mira Talhan (Karna). They are close friends with the prince of Mahoba, Brahma (Arjuna). Together, they go on many adventures that earn them the admiration of Bela (Draupadi), the princess of Delhi. Their adventures also earn them the envy of her father Prithviraj (Duryodhana), whose mind is poisoned by his brother-in-law Mahil (Shakuni) and his commander Chaunra (Drona). Impressed by Alha's skills, Prithviraj offers him the hand of Bela, but Alha, deferring to his lower status, states that a princess should marry a prince—Brahma of Mahoba. But Prithviraj has no desire to send his daughter to Mahoba, a kingdom with which he has an old feud. A series of events results in the death of Brahma and Alha's brothers. Alha avenges their death, but eventually renounces the world, and turns into a jogi—a student of Gorakhnath. He learns the power of forgiveness and uses his power to resurrect Prithviraj, who has to defend India against the attack of Muhammad of Ghor.

In both the stories, we find fathers reluctant to marry their daughters to unsuitable grooms. In both the stories, we find disputes over caste status, land, cattle, jewels, and taxes. In both the stories, we find wisdom and forgiveness bestowed through renunciation, embodied in Gorakhnath—the teacher of the nath-sampradaya—who became very popular in rural India around the tenth century CE. The nath-jogis were worshippers of Datta, considered the teacher of teachers—a form that merged the Hindu trinity, Brahma, Vishnu and Shiva. They valorized renunciation, celibacy, and believed in magical powers (siddhi) that were acquired when women, and all things worldly, were shunned.

VII

Retelling

In which we explore how the two epics were retold in the Buddhist and Jain worlds, by Sanskrit playwrights, as well as regional writers in Southeast Asia, during medieval and modern times.

43

Both epics have Buddhist retellings

Buddha's followers believed that a prince called Siddhartha of the Sakya clan became the Buddha because of karma accumulated in past lives. Tales of his illustrious past lives were compiled as the Jataka tales and narrated by Buddhist monks. In these tales, we discover the Buddhist retelling of parts of the story that Hindus know as the *Ramayana* and the *Mahabharata*.

In the *Dasharatha Jataka*, Dasharatha, king of Varanasi, fears that his ambitious junior queen will harm his eldest son, Ram-Pandita, or Ram, the wise. He consults astrologers who tell him that he will live for twelve years. So, he summons Ram and tells him to go and stay in the forest—where he will be safe from the machinations of the junior queen—and return after twelve years. Ram does as he is asked. But as luck would have it, Dasharatha dies in nine years' time, pining for Ram, and Bharat goes to bring Ram back to the city. 'I promised my father that I would stay in the forest for twelve years so I cannot return earlier,' says Ram. Bharat returns home with Ram's footwear (paduka), which he places on the throne, and begins ruling Ayodhya as Ram's regent until Ram's return. In this story, Ram is described as having integrity and being stoic, as he does not break down upon learning of his father's death. This is because he is the Bodhisattva—fully aware that all things in this world, his father included, are impermanent.

In the *Ghata Jataka*, Ghata-deva is the younger brother of Vasudeva, who is the Buddhist Krishna. Vasudeva and his nine brothers are born to Devibhagga and Upasagara. At birth, they are exchanged for the ten daughters of Devibhagga's maid, Nandagopa. The ten brothers grow up not as princes, but as servants. They grow fond of wrestling and are much feared in the city, for they snatch clothes from the washerman and garlands from the flower seller. They wrestle and defeat everyone, including the royal wrestlers, Chanura and Mustika, and eventually are challenged to a duel by Kamsa. Vasudeva ends up killing his own maternal uncle using a wheel, thus, fulfilling an ancient prophecy. The ten brothers conquer the world and even capture the mysterious floating city of Dvaravati. Then, one day, Vasudeva's son dies. Vasudeva clings to his son's corpse, refusing to let go, until his younger brother, Ghata-deva, intervenes and begs him to fetch the hare from the moon. Vasudeva tells Ghata-deva that his yearning is absurd, and Ghata-deva replies, 'Not as absurd as the yearning to bring your dead son back to life.' Wisdom dawns upon Vasudeva and he comes to terms with his son's death. Later, members of his clan kill each other following a drunken brawl. His brother, Baladeva, dies at the hands of a monster, reborn as a wrestler, and he dies at the hands of Jara, the hunter.

In the Buddhist retelling, Krishna is not as noble, polished and regal as Ram. He is bucolic and violent. There is no mention of the Pandavas in this story. It is interesting to note that many Buddhist caves in India, carved about 2,000 years ago, are often identified by locals as caves built by the Pandavas during their exile. Such is the case in Pandav-leni at Nashik, Maharashtra; Pancha-marhi, Madhya Pradesh; and Rivona caves, Goa. It is in a Buddhist cave at Bhaja near Mumbai, carved 2,200 years ago, that we find the first images of Surya on a chariot and Indra on an elephant.

44

Both epics have Jain retellings

Like Buddhists, Jains too rejected Vedic rituals. Similar to Buddhists, Jain rejected the idea of a god who creates the world and determines our destiny. Unlike Buddhists, however, Jains believe in a permanent soul (jiva) that is bound to the material realm because of karma. They believe that austerities and purification can rid the body of karma, enabling the soul to rise to heaven and gain wisdom and liberation.

Also, unlike Buddhists, Jains did not have one founder-leader. They saw their faith as eternal (sanatan), with 24 great sages—the Tirthankaras—appearing in each of the infinite cycles of this world that has no beginning (anadi) and no end (ananta). Besides the Tirthankaras, each era is blessed with 12 great emperors, the Chakravartis, and 9 non-violent heroes, the Baladevas, whose violent brothers, the Vasudevas, fight villains, the Prati-Vasudeva. Ram, for the Jains, was a non-violent Baladeva, and Krishna was a violent Vasudeva. This makes the *Ramayana* and the *Mahabharata* as much a part of Jain faith as they are of Hindu faith.

Ayodhya, also known as Saket, the sacred city of the *Ramayana*, is an important city for Jains. It is home to five Tirthankaras of the current cycle—the first, Rishabha-nath; the second, Ajita-nath; the fourth, Abhinandan-nath; the fifth, Sumati-nath; and the fourteenth, Ananta-nath. Of the 24 Tirthankaras, 22 belong to the Ikshavaku dynasty, which is Ram's dynasty. Ajita-nath's son, Sagara, was a Chakravarti, and an ancestor of Ram. Vimalasuri, Gunabhadra and Sanghadasa are some of the writers of the Jain *Ramayanas*. The Jain versions vary in many ways from Hindu *Ramayanas*. Some of the variations include:

- Ramayana is often called *Paumacharita*, or the 'legend of Padma', which is the Jain name for Ram.

- Dasharatha was once the king of Varanasi and later moved to Saket (Ayodhya).

- In some versions, Sita is the daughter of Ravana and Mandodari, who was found and raised by Janaka. In others, Sita has a twin-brother, Bhamandala, who is abducted as an infant, and grows up to be a king. He meets, falls in love with, and tries to abduct Sita, but then turns into a monk when he realizes she is his sister.

- Ram goes into forest exile as he feels sorry for Kaikeyi whose son wants to become a monk. When Ram leavs the palace, Bharat is forced to stay back and take care of the city and his mother.

- Ravana is a Vidyadhara and does not have ten heads. He has a necklace with nine pearls that reflect his head nine times, giving the impression that he has ten heads.

- The Vanaras are not monkeys but tribes who have the image of the monkey on their flags.

- Ravana is a devotee of Munisuvirat, the twentieth Jain Tirthankara.

- It is Lakshman who kills Ravana, as Ram prefers non-violence. For this act, he is cast in hell for a long duration.

- When Sita steps into the fire to prove her chastity, the fire turns into a lake and she becomes a Jain nun.

- Ravana will be reborn in a future era as a Tirthankara. During this future life, Sita will be born as his Ganadhara or chief disciple.

The Jain *Mahabharatas*, such as Jinasena's *Harivamsa*, focus less on the Pandavas and more on the battle between Krishna and Jarasandha.

- Krishna's father, Vasudeva, is a very handsome man whose wanderings and amorous liaisons constitute the stories of an epic, the *Vasudevahindi*.

- Krishna's mother, Devaki, gives birth to eight sons. The first six are replaced with the stillborn children of a merchant's wife. The six brothers of Krishna eventually become Jain monks. The seventh and eighth sons are sent to cowherd families and raised as cowherds.

- Krishna's cousin is Neminatha, the twenty-second Tirthankara, who becomes a monk, as he is unable to bear the sounds of animals brought to be slaughtered for his wedding feast.

- In their previous life, the Pandavas were five brothers and they did not stop the wife of the third brother from poisoning a Jain monk; this is why they were reborn as brothers addicted to the vice of gambling. The wife of the third brother was reborn as Draupadi.

- Draupadi has only one husband, Arjuna. She treats Yudhishthira and Bhima, who are elder to Arjuna, as her fathers and Nakula and Sahadeva, who are younger to Arjuna, as her sons. The garland she places around Arjuna breaks and a few flowers fall on the other four brothers, leading to the gossip that she is the common wife of all five brothers.

- The Pandavas gamble and lose their kingdom to the Kauravas and as part of the agreement spend twelve years in the forest and the thirteenth in hiding, disguised as servants in the palace of King Virata. Kichaka who tries to molest Draupadi is punished by Bhima who does not kill him. Kichaka becomes a Jain monk and is eventually liberated.

- The five Pandavas come to Krishna for help against the hundred

Kauravas who have declared war against them. Krishna promises to help them if they help him fight Jarasandha.

- During the war against Jarasandha and the Kauravas, Jarasandha hurls a wheel at Krishna but Nemi-natha stands in the way. This makes the wheel goes around the two cousins, and it eventually sits on Krishna's finger. Krishna then hurls the wheel at Jarasandha and kills him.

- For causing so much bloodshed, Krishna goes to hell, but in a future life, he is born as a Tirthankara. Balarama, his brother, stays non-violent.

- The Pandavas become Jain monks after the war with the Kauravas. While they are meditating, Duryodhana's son, Yavrodhana, puts hot iron chains around the Pandavas' necks, burning their bodies. By then, with the power of meditation, they are so detached from their bodies that they do not suffer; instead, their souls rise to heaven. In some versions, Nakul and Sahadeva are slightly distracted and so their liberation is delayed by a lifetime.

- A hunter called Jaratkumar accidentally kills Krishna. Balaram is inconsolable in his grief and refuses to let go of Krishna's corpse. Then, he sees a man pouring water on a stone, in the hope that it will bloom into lotus flowers. He realizes his foolishness, cremates Krishna's body, and becomes a monk.

- So distracting is Balarama's beauty that a woman, rather than tying a rope around her pot, ties it around the neck of her son. A king is so terrified by Balarama's blazing asceticism that he sends his soldiers to kill him, but lions materialize from thin air to protect him—which is why Balarama comes to be known as Narasimha.

- Kansa does not kill Krishna's sister, Ekanasa, but breaks her nose so that she remains a spinster and does not marry a man who can threaten his rule. Ekanasa becomes a Jain nun after Balarama's sons make fun of her for admiring herself in a mirror. In the forest, some hunters see her meditating and are struck by her beauty. They conclude she is a goddess. They offer her fruits and flowers. When they return they find a pool of blood. Unbeknownst to them, Ekanasa has been attacked and killed by a lion whose bite she bears stoically as she had outgrown all attachment to her body. The hunters assume that the goddess preferes to eat animals rather than fruits and flowers, and so, they begin worshipping her as the blood-drinking, lion-riding, fierce Goddess Durga.

45

Both inspired Sanskrit plays

For a long time, Sanskrit was the language of the gods, known mainly to Brahmins who used it to compose hymns, and explain rituals and the underlying metaphysics. However, in time, Sanskrit became the language of kings. For a thousand years, from

300 CE to 1300 CE, it served as the court language, not just in South Asia but also in Southeast Asia, as far as Vietnam and Cambodia. Once Islam arrived via Persia and Central Asia, Persian became the court language. English eventually replaced Persian, 200 years ago, when the British controlled the subcontinent.

During the age of imperial Sanskrit, many plays were written by playwrights such as Bhasa (300 CE), Kalidasa (500 CE) and Bhavabhuti (700 CE), based on plots from the *Ramayana* and the *Mahabharata*. The retellings value royal intrigue more than divinity. Ram is a noble king. Krishna is a shrewd statesman. Neither is God on earth.

In these plays, for the first time, we find stories where the storyteller argues a point of view like a lawyer, justifying certain actions over others. For example, in Bhasa's *Pratima Nataka*, Kaikeyi's actions are justified, while in Bhasa's *Urubhangam* (The Broken Thigh), Duryodhana is presented as a noble king who regrets his actions.

We find in Bhavabhuti's *Mahaviracharitra* (Tale of a Noble Character), many innovative plots, like Ram and Sita meeting before their marriage at the ashram of Vishamitra, or Ravana's minister, Malyavana, quoting Kautilya's *Artha-shastra* and using various tricks to get Parashurama and Vali to fight Ram. Vali is eventually killed in a fair fight, and he advises Ram to take Sugriva's help. In Bhavabhuti's *Uttara-rama-charita* (Later Life of Ram), we find another innovation—Sita's father Janaka and Ram's mother Kaushalya have a conversation in the hermitage of Valmiki, while Luv and Kush battle Ram's army over the royal horse. In Bhaskara's *Unmatta Raghava* (Lovesick Ram), written in the fourteenth century, Sita accidentally wanders into a grove where she turns into a gazelle. Unable to find her anywhere, Ram pines for her, until Agastya arrives and tells him of Sita's tryst with the grove cursed by Rishi Durvasa.

In Bhasa's *Pancharatram* (The Five Nights), Drona tries to mediate between the Kauravas and Pandavas by seeking as fee half of Duryodhana's land for the Pandavas, for a ritual he conducts for Duryodhana. Duryodhana agrees provided Drona can find the whereabouts of the Pandavas, who are in hiding, within five nights, hence the title of the play. In Bhasa's *Dutavakyam*, Krishna's weapons—the sword Nandaka and the disc Sudarshana—appear as characters.

Roughly around the same time as Bhavabhuti, Bhattanarayana wrote *Venisamharam* (The Braiding of Draupadi's Hair), a play that focuses on rage and violence, and how Bhima manages to tie Draupadi's unbound hair after washing it with Kaurava blood. There is no role of Krishna here. The themes of the play are masculine emotions of heroism (vira) and rage (raudra), even disgust (vibhitsa) and love (shringara), but not at all the veneration or adoration of the divine (bhakti).

Bhasa's plays on the Ramayana	Bhasa's plays on the Mahabharata
Pratima-nataka (The Statues)	*Pancharatram* (The Five Nights)
Yagna Phalam (The Fruit of Ritual)	*Madhyama-vyayoga* (The Middle One)
Abhisheka-nataka (The Coronation)	*Duta-Ghatotkacha* (Ghatokacha as Envoy)
	Dutavakyam (The Envoy's Message)
	Urubhangam (The Broken Thigh)
	Karnabharam (Karna's Burden)
	Harivamsa or *Bala-charita* (Hari's Dynasty or The Tale of Childhood)

46

Both spread beyond Indian shores

In the fifteenth century, Thailand's capital was a city called Ayutthaya, which is Ayodhya in the local language. When Burmese soldiers overran this city in the eighteenth century, a new king rose. He called himself Rama I. He established the city we now know as Bangkok, wrote the epic *Ramakien*—which is *Ramayana* in the local language—made it the national epic, and had stories from it painted as murals on the walls of the temple of the Emerald Buddha, patronized by the royal family. Though he was a Buddhist, the king established his royal credentials by identifying himself with the mythical Ram.

In those days, the lines between Buddhism and Hinduism were not as stark as they are now. Ram was as much a hero for the Buddhists of Southeast Asia as he was for the Hindus of South Asia. Soon, he became a role model for local kings. This legitimizing of kingship through the *Ramayana* began more than a thousand years ago. In a stone inscription from Burma in the Mon language, dating to the eleventh century, King Kyanzittha of the Bagan dynasty proclaimed that in his previous life he was a close relative of Rama of Ayodhya. In the Angkor Wat ruins, built in twelfth-century Cambodia, in a fifty-metre-long corridor adjacent to the one depicting the royal procession, one finds carved episodes from *Ramaker*, the Khmer retelling of the

Ramayana. Murals based on the *Ramayana* can also be found on the walls of the royal palace complex in Phnom Penh.

The *Ramayana* was clearly more popular than the *Mahabharata*, as indicated by cultural references from it that can be found in almost every country in Southeast Asia. This can be because of its role in establishing kingship. The *Ramayanas* in Southeast Asia have many plot variations. For example, in Thailand, Hanuman is the hero and is more monkey-like and aggressive, lacking the grace attributed to him in Indian temples. Most disconcerting to the devout Indian Hindu is watching the Southeast Asian Hanuman behaving like a mischievous rake who enchants women, including Ravana's sister, Surpanakha, and his wife, Mandodari. One of the most common stories told is of how Hanuman charms and changes the mind of Suvarnamaccha, the mermaid daughter of Ravana, who steals the rocks used by the monkeys to build a bridge to Lanka. In another story, he outwits Vibhishana's daughter, Benjkaya, a sorceress who takes the form of Sita's corpse to make Ram turn back. The Malaysian *Hikayat Seri Rama* gives more importance to the decisive Lakshman and is more sympathetic to Ravana, while making Ram aloof and imperious at the same time.

Indonesia is perhaps the only country where it is the *Mahabharata* that gains prominence. It is retold with many local variations as part of the island nation's famous Wayang shadow puppetry. In the *Kakawin Ramayana* of Java, the first part of the story is true to Valmiki's *Ramayana*, but it is the second part that is more popular, as it deals with the adventures of the local comic hero, the misshapen guardian-god Semar and his three odd sons. It is in the islands of Bali, Sumatra and Java of Indonesia that the *Mahabharata*, known locally as *Bharatayudha*, is clearly as important, if not more. In one plot, Krishna and Arjuna meet Ram and Lakshman, and Ram takes the help of Arjuna to build the bridge to Lanka. At the modern Bali airport, we find a grand image of Ghatotkacha jumping on the horses of Karna's chariot.

The epics reached Southeast Asia via Odia and Tamil sea merchants who took advantage of the monsoon winds to make annual trips there. They exchanged goods and shared stories. It is said that at night, the ship's cloth sails, illuminated by lamps, inspired the storytellers to create the art of leather shadow puppet theatre, which explains why shadow puppetry continues to thrive along the Coromandel sea coasts of India and across most of Southeast Asia, for example, as Ravan-chhaya in Odisha and Wayang in Indonesia.

Direct transmission stopped approximately a thousand years ago, the same time Buddhism waned in India, and sea travel became a taboo, with Hindus fearing that it would pollute them and result in a loss of caste. Trade was outsourced to Arab sea merchants who also spread Islam to Southeast Asia. We can be quite sure of this because the *Ramayana* found in Southeast Asia lacks the bhakti flavour so integral to the Indian *Ramayana*, first made explicit in the ninth-century, Tamil *Kamba Ramayana*. What is clear in the *Ramayana* and the *Mahabharata* that prevail in Southeast Asia is a greater emphasis on the drama and very little focus on the philosophy.

In Malaysia, we find the story of the *Mahabharata* retold as *Hikayat Pandawa Jaya*, focusing on the battle between the Pandavas and Kauravas. The story of Krishna is additionally told in Malayasia as *Hikayat Sang Samba*, where the story of Krishna, his father Vasudeva, and his son Samba are narrated. Images of Krishna killing demons are found in the temples of Angkor

Wat in Cambodia, and in Prambanan in Indonesia. What is characteristic by its absence is the romantic cowherd Krishna who became popular in India during the Bhakti Age. This reaffirms the theory that the transmission of Hinduism to Southeast Asia stopped around the time Islam entered India.

Initially, Buddhism overshadowed Hinduism in Southeast Asia. Later, Islam overshadowed Buddhism, especially in islands connected to trade routes, such as Malaysia and Indonesia; less so in Burma, Cambodia and Thailand. By the sixteenth century, these countries struggled to preserve older stories since all things pre-Islamic were seen as jahila, or ignorance, by clerics. And so, in the Malaysian retellings of the *Ramayana* and the *Mahabharata*, we find clear disclaimers that pay lip service to Islamic law, stating that the stories retold are untrue.

	Ramayana	Mahabharata
Indonesia	Ramakavaca	Bharatayudha
Malaysia	Hikayat Seri Ram	Hikayat Pandawa Jaya
Cambodia	Ramkear	
Thailand	Ramakien	
Laos	Phra Lak Phra Lam	
Burma	Yamayana	

47

Both inspired regional forms

Most people in India are not familiar with the Sanskrit *Ramayana* or the *Mahabharata*. We read popular versions, based on regional retellings, which first appeared less than 1,000 years ago. They became widely prevalent from around 500 years ago.

As we have seen, the *Ramayana*, with its linear narrative, was clearly more popular than the more complex *Mahabharata*. *Ramayana* had more scope for heroism, romance and tragedy whereas the *Mahabharata*, with its focus on the division of property and the death of brothers, was shunned as inauspicious. Since Krishna-bhakti peaked, people preferred hearing stories of Krishna's childhood in the *Bhagavata* over stories of Krishna's adulthood and death found in the *Mahabharata*. We find the translations emerging from south to north, mirroring the doctrine of Bhakti that also spread from south to the north.

Below is a sampling of regional retellings of the *Ramayana* and the *Mahabharata*. Note that these are not the earliest works, but the most popular or the most comprehensive works. Many of the earlier works are either lost (for instance, the fifteenth-century Bengali *Mahabharata*, *Bharat Panchali*, composed by Shrikara) or episodic (seventeenth-century Gujarati akhyanas of Premananda), covering one of the many tales of the epic.

Language	Ramayana	Mahabharata
Tamil	Kamban in the tenth century (*Iramavataram*)	Villiputturar in the fourteenth century
Malayalam	Thunchaththu Ramanujan Ezhuthachan in the sixteenth century (*Adhyatma Ramayana*)	Thunchaththu Ramanujan Ezhuthachan in the sixteenth century
Kannada	Kumara Valmiki in the sixteenth century (*Torave Ramayana*)	Naranappa (Kumara Vyasa) in the fifteenth century
Telugu	Gona Budda Reddy in the thirteenth century (*Ranganatha Ramayana*)	Nannaya Bhattaraka in the eleventh century
Odia	Balaram Das in the sixteenth century (*Dandi Ramayana*)	Sarala Das in the fifteenth century
Bengali	Krittibasa in the fifteenth century	Kavi Sanjay in the fifteenth century
Assamese	Madhava Kandali in the fourteenth century	Kaviratna Sarasvati in the fourteenth century
Marathi	Eknath in sixteenth century (*Bhavaratha Ramayana*)	Mukteshwara in the seventeenth century
Gujarati	Giridhar in the eighteenth century	Bhalan in the fifteenth century (akhyanas based on various episodes)
Hindi	Tulsidas in the sixteenth century (*Ramcharitmanas*) in Awadhi language	Vishnudas in the fifteenth (*Pandavcharit*) in Gwalior Brijbhasa

Regional retellings are not translations, or faithful reproductions, but rather innovative retellings. Even though they are structurally faithful to the Sanskrit work, they have many deviations. For example, the Bengali *Ramayana*, by Krittibas, contains the first reference to the Lakshman Rekha and the dhobi gossiping about Sita's reputation. In the Kannada *Ramayana* we find the tale of Ravana being unable to lift Shiva's bow, and so not being able to marry Sita, while in the Malayalam *Ramayana* we find the story of Ravana probably being Sita's father. Sarala Das in his Odia *Mahabharata* tells the backstory of Shakuni—how his family was killed by Duryodhana—which makes Shakuni not the epic villain, but the epic victim, who hated the Kauravas.

Many of these works shift the geography of the tale—Balarama Das makes Ram visit Puri in Odisha, while Villiputturar makes Ajuna visit Srirangam in Tamil Nadu. Most regional retellings seek to establish the divinity of Ram and Krishna for they were composed at the time when bhakti, or passionate devotion, was the dominant expression of Hinduism. So, it is not surprising to see that preference is given either to the upright Ram, or the lovable child Krishna of the *Bhagavata*, than to the more complex, adult Krishna of the *Mahabharata*. These works are conscious of being holy books—retellings of the exploits of venerable characters. They are not meant to be secular entertainment, a trend prevalent in the Sanskrit plays.

48

Both have inspired novels since the nineteenth century

From the eighteenth century onwards, the novel as a literary form became popular in Europe and it fired the imagination of Indian authors after it was introduced to India in the nineteenth century. Indian authors began writing novels based on the *Ramayana* and the *Mahabharata*. In these novels, unlike in the regional retellings of the *Ramayana* and the *Mahabharata*, there is no desire by the author to be self-consciously pious. The story is told either by the all-seeing storyteller/narrator or through the eyes of a particular character, often playing the role of a lawyer or judge, defending the case of one character, while prosecuting others. There is a strong urge to connect the ancient tale to everyday modern experience. This has led to the rise of a genre known as 'mythological fiction', popular in both regional languages, as well as in English, in prose, as well as in poetry.

On the one hand are authors who use the critique of the story from a feminist or Marxist perspective to affirm how the epics were used to enforce Brahminical hegemony. On the other hand are authors who tell the story as proto-history, presenting their imagination as Vedic history and truth.

	Ramayana	Mahabharata
Gujarati	*Rame Sitane Maryan Jo!* by Pannalal Patel	*Krishnavatar* by Kanhaiyalal Munshi
Marathi	*Shyamini* by Tara Varanase (on Surpanakha)	*Mrityunjaya* by Shivaji Sawant (on Karna)
Hindi	*Abhyudaya* by Narendra Kohli	*Rashmirathi* a poem by Ramdhari Singh Dinar (on Karna)
English	*Asura* by Anand *Neelakanthan* (on Ravana)	*Palace of Illusions* by Chitra Divakuruni Banerjee (on Draupadi)
Odia	*Nirbasita* by Kalia Panigrahi (on Sita)	*Jagyaseni* by Prativa Ray (on Draupadi)
Bengali	*Meghanada-vadha* by Michael Madhusudana Dutta (on Indrajit)	*Panchojonno* by Gajendrakumar Mitra
Assamese	*Dashorothir Khuj* by Indira Goswami	*Maharothi* by Chandra Prasad Saikia
Tamil	*Apoorva Ramayanam* by Thiruppur Krishnan (on Bharata)	*Venmurasu* by Jeyamohan
Kannada	*Ramayana Darshanam,* a poem by Kuvempu	*Parva* by Bhyrappa
Malayalam	*Oorukaval* by Sarah Joseph (on Angada)	*Randamoozham* by M. T. Vasudevan Nair (on Bhima)
Telugu	*Janaki Vimukti* by Muppala Ranganayakamma	*Draupadi* by Yarlagadda Lakshmi Prasad

It is significant that in the Bhakti period, people preferred the *Ramayana* over the *Mahabharata* and there was a great desire to show both Ram and Krishna as embodiments of perfection. In the novel-writing modern times, there is a greater preference for the *Mahabharata* over the *Ramayana*, and the desire to find faults in both Ram and Krishna—more flawed humans and less perfect gods. While ancient Sanskrit plays are not devotional, at no point are Ram and Krishna seen as problematic in these plays; something that emerges through the lens of modern writers.

VIII

Wisdom

In which we explore how the two epics enabled Hindus to appreciate complex ideas such as karma, dharma, diversity, equality, infinity and impermanence.

49

Both epics speak of actions and reactions

The Hindu world is based on karma. Karma means action as well as reaction. Every action is essentially a reaction to past events. And every action in the present, results in a reaction in the future, that one is obliged to experience—if not in this life then in the next. This makes rebirth—punar-janma—central to the idea of karma.

The idea of karma was explained in the *Ramayana* and the *Mahabharata* in two ways—first, by using boons and curses, and second, by showing how every story is a subset of a larger story. Thus, we learn that there is always something before the beginning and something after the end.

Since the *Ramayana* came before the *Mahabharata*, it almost seems like the *Ramayana* is the action to which the *Mahabharata* is the reaction. Take the story of the rivalry between Indra, the rain god, and Surya, the sun god. In the *Ramayana*, Ram supports Surya's son, Sugriva, in his fight against Indra's son, Vali. Ram shoots Vali and enables Sugriva to become king. In the *Mahabharata*, Krishna supports Indra's son, Arjuna, in his rivalry against Surya's son, Karna. Krishna enables Arjuna to defeat Karna. Vali is shot unfairly, while Sugriva distracts him. Likewise, Karna is shot unfairly, while he is trying to release the wheel of his chariot that is stuck in the mud. In isolation, each story seems unjustified and imbalanced. Seen together, the two stories counter and complete each other.

In the *Ramayana*, Ram rides on Hanuman's shoulders. In the *Mahabharata*, Hanuman rides on the flag that flutters above Arjuna's chariot for which Krishna serves as a charioteer. Thus in the *Ramayana*, Hanuman carries Vishnu in the form of Ram, while in the *Mahabharata*, Vishnu, as Krishna, carries Hanuman atop his chariot. A balance is thus maintained.

Many of the promises made by Ram in the *Ramayana* are fulfilled in the *Mahabharata*. Ram tells the rishis and rishikas of the forest that he cannot spend time with them, as he can only spend time with Sita, but he promises to be their companion as Krishna when they take birth as gopikas in their next life. Likewise, Ram fulfils Jambhavan's desire to wrestle with him as Krishna. There are folk stories from Karnataka about how monkeys hired by Naraka-asura refused to fight Krishna, for they recognized him as Ram. Thus, the two epics are deeply interconnected.

When we read the *Vishnu Purana*, we further realize that both the *Ramayana* and the *Mahabharata* are reactions to a cosmic event. We learn that Vishnu once helped the devas fight the asuras. The asuras went to their guru, Shukra, but he was away. So they hid behind his mother, who protected them until Vishnu hurled his wheel—the Sudarshan Chakra—and beheaded Shukra's mother. For this heinous act, Shukra cursed Vishnu that he would be born on earth as a mortal—as Ram and Krishna. So the birth of Ram and Krishna can be seen as the fulfilment of a curse.

In another story, four sages known as the Sanat Kumars visit Vishnu at his abode, Vaikuntha, located on the ocean of milk. But they are stopped by the doorkeepers, Jaya and Vijaya, on the grounds that Vishnu is asleep. This happens several times until the Sanat Kumars get irritated and they curse the doorkeepers that they will be born on earth as demons. So Jaya and Vijaya are born on earth as Ravana and Kumbhakarna, and as Shishupala and Dantavakra. Jaya and Vijaya wonder why they have been cursed for doing their duty as doorkeepers. Vishnu consoles them and promises to liberate them himself by ensuring their return to Vaikuntha. To make sure Vishnu comes down from Vaikuntha to liberate them, Jaya and Vijaya behave very badly during their stay on earth. Ravana and Kumbhakarna, Shishupala and Dantavakra, spend all their time making the lives of humans miserable, forcing humans to pray to Vishnu and beg him to intervene. This behaviour is called viprit-bhakti, or reverse devotion, where the hatred and rage of a devotee is an expression of his love for God. In response, Vishnu takes the form of Ram to kill Ravana and Kumbhakarna, and the form of Krishna to kill Shishupala and Dantavakra.

Through the stories of Vishnu, Ram and Krishna, we learn how the past telescopes into the present and how the present telescopes into the future. We also learn how events are not shaped by a single factor; there are many things that contribute to shaping an event. So the world remains a mystery.

One must be wary of Western/modern understandings of karma that are deliberate misunderstandings created in order to discredit Hindu thought. Thus, you find people who equate karma with fatalism. The doctrine of karma says you cannot control present circumstances, but you can choose your reaction to them. This is not fatalism. The doctrine of karma also says that you contribute to the creation of your circumstances. This is also not fatalism; in fact, it prevents you from wallowing in self-pity and the blame game—it makes you take responsibility for your life. When Ram is exiled to the forest, he knows it is karma—not fate, but the outcome of past deeds. When Jarasandha burns the city of Mathura, Krishna knows this is karma—not fate but the outcome of his act of killing Kamsa, Jarasandha's son-in-law. There is no point blaming oneself or others for it. There is no point playing the victim, for we contributed to the creation of the event. All one can do is respond responsibly.

Then there are those who equate karma to the biblical concept of 'as you sow, so shall you reap'. This assumes misfortune is the result of bad deeds performed in the past. This moral understanding of karma does not take into account the complexities of karma. We don't function in isolation; our karma is like one tree in a forest of karmas, and so our karma is impacted by other people's karma. The fate of a tree in the forest is determined not only by its own capability and capacity, but also by the behaviour of the plants around it. So our fortune and misfortune are not just a function of our deeds. Ram's forest exile is a function of his father's deeds; he has no say in the matter. It is not his 'seed' that creates this unfortunate 'fruit'. That is why Krishna in the Gita tells Arjuna to focus on action (seed), not results (fruit).

50

Both epics draw attention to the idea of infinity

If Buddhism gave value to the concept of nothingness or zero (shunya), Hinduism gave value to its opposite, the concept of everything-ness or infinity (ananta). While we can experience the absence of a thing, we cannot experience the presence of everything; we can only indicate what infinity means—another chance, another possibility, another explanation, by continuously speaking of recursion and fractals. We see this in the *Ramayana* and the *Mahabharata*.

The *Ramayana* is incomplete without the *Mahabharata*. Events in the *Ramayana* make sense when we appreciate the events of the *Mahabharata*. Both epics make sense only when we read the *Vishnu Purana* and realize that Ram and Krishna function as subsets of Vishnu, which in turn adds up when we read the story of Shiva in the *Shiva Purana*. This is substantiated when we read about insecure Brahma and his insecure sons in the *Brahma Purana*, which is further explained when we encounter nature as Devi in the *Devi Purana*. Nature, as we know, is boundless, extending beyond the horizon. No king can hope to conquer all. A chakra-varti, master of the wheel, can have empires stretching up to the horizon only, where his eyes can see—not beyond. Who sees it all?

The Puranas make no sense unless we appreciate the Vedas. Hinduism makes no sense unless we appreciate the monasticism of Buddhism and Jainism. We realize how Hinduism values the soul (jiva) and God (parmatma), Jainism values only the soul, not God, and Buddhism values neither—but all three value rebirth and karma.

In Jainism, monasteries were built on top of mountains with the image of the Tirthankara staring into the horizon in all four directions. This chatur-mukha image was presented in Hinduism as Brahma, the creator. But while the Jain image is that of a wise man, in Hinduism, it was the form of God. The infinitely expanded mind of Jainism was seen as divine in Hinduism. Thus, we find resonance between Hinduism and Jainism, even though the former is more worldly, and the latter more monastic. Song and dance, which are key components of Hindu worship, are shunned in Jain practice, which prefers silence and stillness. Every concept in India has a complement and alternative, creating infinite possibilities.

In each episode of the *Ramayana* and the *Mahabharata*, we get access to limitless wisdom. In the *Mahabharata*, for example, Krishna repeatedly shows his infinite form—his mother sees the whole world in his mouth; Arjuna sees his universal form in the battlefield of Kurukshetra. Yet, Krishna's life is finite and his actions take place only in a finite space around the Gangetic plains. He is finite, yet contains infinity, and is aware of infinity.

Krishna's opposite is also true, and needs to be considered and contained in the stories. So, unlike Krishna, Ram has no awareness of his divinity and his infinity, even though he is a form of Vishnu. This is critical, for Ravana cannot be killed by a being who knows he is divine. Only a finite being, a mortal, can kill him. Ram not knowing he is infinite has value; Krishna knowing he is infinite also has value. Both contribute to the establishment of dharma—Ram unknowingly, Krishna knowingly.

Thus, infinity is located in a part of the story and embodied in the whole story. Infinity is within the boundaries as well as beyond the boundaries. All things exist as a fractal. All things are recursive, a function of the self—be it the Vedas, or the Puranas, or the epics, or life itself.

51

Both epics differentiate between territory and property

Hindu philosophy cannot be understood without discussing matsya-nyaya, or fish justice—the Vedic phrase for the law of the jungle. The first reference to matsya-nyaya can be found in the *Shatapatha Brahamana*, composed 3,000 years ago. Written a thousand years later, in both the *Artha-shastra* and *Manu-smriti*, we learn that kings were appointed by the gods to ensure that humans did not behave like animals, and claim 'territory' rather than respecting 'property'.

In the jungle, might is right. The strong claim territory for food and to mate, and push away the weak—as Vali does in Kishkindha and Ravana does in Lanka. Animals cannot bequeath titles and kingdoms to their children. Culture creates the concept of property. It becomes an extension of the self. In culture, your value is based on what you own. You are a function of your property. We often assume that Ayodhya is Ram's property and Hastinapur is Yudhishthira's property when, in fact, it is their responsibility. A king exists, as per Hindu philosophy, only to ensure that *other people's property* is safe. The desire for property, the attachment to property, the craving for other people's property— all are indicators of insecurity, failure to recognize atma, and to be consumed by aham.

The fight over property is essentially a fight for what is 'mine'. For what is 'mine' defines what is 'me'. So, essentially, it is a fight for identity. As humans, we are struggling to know who we are. We establish our identity through property and civilization evolves to protect this property. This identity, based on property, is ego (aham)—a manifestation of insecurity. With wisdom and hindsight, we discover that true identity is not dependent on property. The true identity of humans is our soul (atma). While aham makes us cling and accumulate, and makes us envious, atma simply observes our fear and traces it to the mortality of the flesh that the atma inhabits. This atma is what the *Rig Veda* refers to as the bird that watches another bird eat fruit. In the Upanishads, this atma is described as something that is present within all organisms (jiva-atma) as well as all around us (brahman, param-atma).

Ram is the embodiment of this atma. So, he is at peace in Ayodhya as well as in the forest. He fights for Sita not because she is 'his' but because he is the defender of his family's reputation. He rules Ayodhya, not because he wants to be the king, but because that is his role as the eldest son of the royal family. As the king, he embodies dharma, overturning the law of the jungle, shunning the desire to dominate and be territorial, which is a manifestation of hunger and fear that plagues all living things (jiva). Only humans—by virtue of imagination (manas)—can overthrow this desire.

Likewise, Krishna is the embodiment of atma who asks Arjuna to fight, not for property, not to seek supremacy over his cousins, not for fame or approval, not to indulge his aham, but for dharma, for social order, and to be a dependable brother who fights to get back the livelihood taken away by his cousins. This can only happen when he accepts the immortality, hence tranquillity, of the atma.

52

Both epics value the stage of life

Traditionally, varna dharma makes no sense without ashrama dharma. However, in the reality of Hindu society, everyone focuses on varna dharma while ashrama dharma is all but forgotten. While varna dharma focuses on one's vocation and station in the society, ashrama dharma focuses on one's stage in life.

As per Vedic society, every human being had to go through four stages in life—as a student (brahmacharya), a householder (grihasta), a retired person (vanaprastha), and finally, a hermit (sanyasa). The idea was to balance the householder's life with the hermit's life—the mundane with the mystical. The idea was also to ensure that the earth was not burdened by too many generations feeding on it—when the new generation arrived (a son got married), the old generation stepped back (a father gradually gave up the reins of his household, a grandfather prepared to become a wandering hermit), thus taking into account that in the society no one is permanent and no one is essential. Through this dynamic flux, stability was maintained.

Both the *Ramayana* and the *Mahabharata* speak of ashrama dharma, but very differently. While the *Ramayana* tries to uphold it, the *Mahabharata* reveals a resistance to it.

In the *Ramayana*, Dasharatha, king of Ayodhya, seeks to maintain ashrama and so prepares to retire as soon as Ram gets married and returns home with a bride. Ram, too, is reminded of his mortality by Yama, the god of death, when his children are old enough to manage the kingdom. And so, after bidding farewell to all, he walks into River Sarayu, which can be seen literally as killing oneself, or metaphorically as giving up the world—even one's identity—and becoming a hermit. By contrast, Ram's adversary, Ravana, the scholar of the Vedas, has grown-up sons with wives of their own, but still refuses to let go of the throne. He is continuously on the lookout for more brides and concubines, with no intention to retire or become a hermit.

In the *Mahabharata*, Bhishma is not married and so should be a hermit. However, he lives as a householder, taking care of his father's young children. He gets them brides. When these brides bear less-than-perfect children, he hangs around, managing Hastinapur, securing brides for his nephews. And when they give birth to a hundred and five children, he still hangs around, as he fears their quarrels will break the household, which is eventually what happens. Even when his grand-nephews have children of their own, and are busy fighting, he leads the Kaurava army in the war against the Pandavas, and tries to create a stalemate, hoping against hope that the family conflict will be resolved. He thus lives an extremely long life, taking full advantage of the boon that allows him to choose the time of his death. He does not want to retire till he sets everything right. In other words, he rejects the ashrama system, believes he is indispensable, and that perfection can be achieved. By contrast, after ruling for thirty-six years, Yudhishthira voluntarily gives up the crown and makes his grand-nephew, Parikshit, son of Abhimanyu, king of Hastinapur and walks up to the Himalayas with his brothers and wife, as a hermit.

53

Both have underlying feminist themes

Patriarchy privileges the male gender over the female, while feminism restores the balance.

In the *Ramayana*, we find chastity used as a device to domesticate women. Sexually aggressive and demanding women such as Kaikeyi and Surpanakha are villains. Women such as Ahalya and Sita are victims, abused by lustful men like Indra and Ravana, and are punished rather than being supported by their husbands, Gautama (who turns Ahalya into stone) and Ram (who banishes Sita), for no fault of theirs.

The *Mahabharata* documents the decline of female agency over four generations. In the first generation, Ganga marries Shantanu only when he promises her complete freedom after marriage. Satyavati marries Shantanu only when she is assured her children will be his heirs. In the second generation, Amba, Ambika and Ambalika are stopped from selecting their own grooms by Bhishma who abducts them for his weakling brother, Vichitravirya. When Vichitravirya dies childless, his widows are forced to allow Vyasa to come to their bed and give them children. In the third generation, Kunti chooses Pandu to be her groom but has to accept Pandu's other wife, Madri, who is bought by the Kuru clan. Gandhari blindfolds herself to share her husband's blindness, and so is declared a sati, or chaste wife. In the fourth generation, five brothers share Draupadi, a decision made not by Draupadi, but by her mother-in-law, Kunti.

There is a tendency to see the *Ramayana* as more patriarchal and the *Mahabharata* as more feminist, since Sita suffers injustice silently while Draupadi screams for justice and the blood of the Kauravas. But a closer look reveals something completely different.

In the *Ramayana*, Sita makes five choices. She may not have chosen her husband but she takes the decision to follow Ram to the forest, and the decision to cross the Lakshman Rekha in order to feed a hungry man. She also takes the decision to not be rescued by Hanuman but wait for Ram instead. It is her decision to return to Ayodhya with Ram although she is given the choice to go wherever she wishes. It is also her choice, finally, to not return to Ayodhya, after Ram banishes her in response to street gossip. Here is a woman who makes her choices. Her children inherit Ram's throne.

In the *Mahabharata*, Draupadi is continuously disappointed in her husbands, especially her favourite, Arjuna. Arjuna, who wins her in an archery contest, shares her with his brothers. All the husbands have many wives who, as per Draupadi's wishes, are not allowed to stay in Indraprastha—the city the Pandavas build for Draupadi. But Arjuna and Krishna trick Draupadi into allowing Subhadra to stay in the palace. The five brothers watch helplessly when Dushasana drags her by the hair and tries to disrobe her in public. They are also helpless when Kichaka slaps her in the court of Virata. Finally, she manipulates Bhima to get her revenge. She gets him to kill Kichaka, and goads him into killing the hundred Kauravas and helping her wash her hair with their blood.

This has resulted in Draupadi being seen as Kali in many folk traditions and Bhima being seen as her Bhairava. Her children die in the war at Kuruskhetra and Subhadra's grandchild inherits the Pandava throne. Draupadi follows her husband when they give up the throne and decide to climb the Himalayas until they reach swarga. But she slips and falls to her death. Yudhishthira advises his younger brothers to not turn back and simply keep walking, for as hermits seeking a place in paradise, they must let go of all attachments and possessions—even their common wife.

But is a wife the property of a husband? Does she have her own agency? These questions are continuously raised in both epics. Ram treats Sita as a woman who can make choices. Draupadi demands to know from the Kurus if a man who has lost himself can still wager his wife. These conversations question the assumed power dynamic between husband and wife in traditional Hindu society. They simmer with feminism.

54

Both refer to the queer

In an attempt to prove that Hinduism is patriarchal and celebrates inequality, many often quote the lines from Tulsidas's *Ram-charit-manas*, composed 400 years ago in Hindi, where Varuna, the sea god, while submitting to the power of Ram, says, '*Dhol ganwar shudra pashu nari sakal taadana ke adhikari*' (the drum, the dumb, the servant, the beast and the woman, need to be beaten to get them to work).

Few speak of another line in the same literary work, spoken by Ram himself, to the storytelling crow Kakabhusandi, '*Purush napunsak nari va jiv charachar koi, sarva bhaav bhaja kapat taji mohi param priya soi*' (man, queer, woman, even plants and animals, free of meanness, full of devotion, are all equally dear to me). This celebrates equality, not just between men and women, but also between humans, plants and animals. The verse also includes the colloquial word for queer, 'napunsak', which literally means 'not quite man'—it can be applied to gay, lesbian, transgender and intersex people.

Maybe it was the familiarity with this verse that led hijras to equate Ram's reign (Ram rajya) with gender equality and inclusion. Hijras are a community of transgendered men in India who choose to castrate themselves as they reject their masculinity.

They are a marginalized community that functions as a caste group, with entry based on initiation via a community leader (guru). Amongst them is a story from the *Ramayana* that grants them legitimacy. They say that when Ram returned from his forest exile he found a group of hijras outside the gates of Ayodhya. They had left the city on the day Ram had left for the forest and had stayed out ever since. When Ram asked the reason for this, they replied, 'You told the men who followed you to return home. You told the women who followed you to return home. You had no instructions for us, who are neither men nor women. So we waited until you returned.' Moved by their devotion, Ram took them by the hand and led them into his city. Ram's rule (Ram rajya) would include all—even the third gender.

Eunuchs or castrated males also play a role in the *Mahabharata*. When Arjuna rejects the sexual advances of the nymph, Urvashi, she curses him that he will lose his manhood. Indra limits the curse and says it will only last for a year—the year depending on Arjuna's choice. So during the thirteenth year of exile, Arjuna hides in the women's quarters in the palace of Virata, king of Matsya, as a eunuch-dancer. He occupies the role traditionally given to hijras.

Hindu scriptures always speak of the third gender. And they are an integral part of mythology. The *Ramayana* and the *Mahabharata* are no exceptions.

Many regional *Ramayanas* speak of how the queer plays a key role in the birth of Vali and Sugriva. Their 'mother' in some stories is Aruna, the charioteer of Surya—the sun god—who takes the form of a woman to see the dance of nymphs (apsaras) in paradise (swarga). In other stories, Riksha, king of Kishkinda, falls into a pond and comes out as a woman. The female form of the male Aruna/Riksha enchants Indra and Surya. So, they make love to her and she bears them a son each—Vali with the rain god, Sugriva with the sun god. Thus, the key characters of the epic are children of men who become women.

If the *Ramayana* speaks of male to female transgenders, then the *Mahabharata* speaks of at least one female to male transgender. Draupadi's elder brother, Shikhandi, turns out to be a woman raised as a man by her father, Drupada, king of Panchala. The discovery is made on the wedding night by Shikhandi's wife who complains to her father, who then threatens to attack and destroy Panchala. Shikhandi wants to kill herself to prevent this from happening and by the grace of a yaksha, called Sthunakarna, obtains male genitalia by which he satisfies courtesans sent by his father-in-law and thus proves his manhood. Bhishma refuses to fight him in battle because he sees her as a woman, for that is her biological gender. Krishna insists Shikhandi is a man, for that is the gender she has chosen. Bhishma lowers his bow and Krishna tells Shikhandi and Arjuna, who stand on his chariot, to fire arrows and kill the patriarch, thus turning the tide of the war at Kurukshetra. That this event takes place on the tenth day of the eighteen-day war, right in the middle, indicates the episode involving the queer is part of the grand design.

At this point, it makes sense to compare the queer as expressed in Hindu mythology with the queer as expressed in Greek mythology. Hindu mythology focuses on gender or body (male to female transformation) while Greek mythology focuses on sexuality or feelings (man-boy love or sex). And so, even today India, is relatively more comfortable with the transgender than the homosexual, whereas Western society is relatively more comfortable with homosexuality than with transgender people.

55

Both challenge ahimsa

Both the *Ramayana* and the *Mahabharata* deal with the issue of violence (himsa) and non-violence (ahimsa). Conventional understanding is that violence is bad, and non-violence is good. Conventional understanding does not take into consideration the purpose of violence in nature. But the Vedas do.

In nature, a living organism (jiva) consumes food. Carnivores eat herbivores, and herbivores eat plants. Life feeds on life. A non-living (a-jiva) or dead (nir-jiva) organism does not consume food. That which is consumed is invariably destroyed. So, the very act of consumption involves violence—destruction. Since plants consume inorganic elements (pancha-maha-bhuta) such as water, air, sunlight and nutrients in the soil, they do not face resistance. However, plants and animals do everything in their power to resist being consumed by animals. No living creature wants to die. In order to survive, plants grow sharp thorns to stop animals from eating them. Bees sting to protect the hive. Snakes strike to protect their eggs. Lions fight to defend their territory from rivals, and prevent access to their mates. Violence enables the prey to defend itself. Violence enables the predator to overcome these defences if it has to find nourishment. Violence, thus, serves the predator and the prey in their quest for survival.

Culture feeds on nature to establish itself. Unless the forest is burnt, fields, orchards and pastures cannot be established. Violence is a key component of human enterprise—the destruction of ecosystems for agriculture, herding and mining. This act provides extra resources for people, and enables humans to concentrate on tasks beyond looking for food. Thus, violence underlies the rise of civilization. We learn this very starkly in the *Mahabharata*, when the building of the city of Indraprastha demands the burning of the forest of Khandava.

Hermits seek to withdraw from society, hence non-violence (ahimsa) is key to monastic discipline. Householders have no escape from violence; it is the burden they have to bear, or outsource to other humans.

The *Ramayana* and the *Mahabharata* are epics for householders, not hermits. Is the discussion on whether violence is good or bad; or is it on which kind of violence is good (dharma) and which kind of violence is bad (adharma)? The answer is simple—violence that enables the survival of the family is good, violence that indulges the ego (aham) is bad.

In the *Ramayana*, Ram is asked to protect rishis from rakshasas. The rishis through yagna are establishing new settlements. The rakshasas oppose this process. Confrontation between the rishis and rakshasas is inevitable. The killing of rakshasas and the protection of rishis is seen as dharma, as rakshasas are seen as creatures who grab resources, while rishis, through the ritual of yagna, exchange resources. The killing of Vali, who does not share his kingdom with Sugriva, is seen as dharma. The killing of Ravana, who locks Sita up in his palace and refuses to let her go back to her husband, is also seen as dharma.

In the *Mahabharata*, Bhima's killing of Baka who torments villagers is seen as dharma. Bhima's killing of Kichaka who abuses Draupadi is seen as dharma. The killing of the Kauravas, who refuse to share even a needlepoint of their land with their cousins, Pandavas, is seen as dharma, for without land how will the Pandavas sustain themselves? Burning another forest to build another city is not acceptable.

Dharma must not be confused with good deeds or punya. Every action—good or bad —has consequences—good and bad. That is karma. And so, even an act of dharma, done to protect the body and the family and to not indulge the ego, has consequences which are not always desirable.

In the *Ramayana*, Lakshman may think that in mutilating, rather than killing the promiscuous Surpanakha, he is doing an act of dharma, but after that incident there is no more happiness in the life of Ram and Sita. They are separated, first by Ravana and then, by gossip in Ayodhya. Such is the working of karma.

Likewise, in the *Mahabharata*, even though Krishna establishes dharma, he invites the curse of Gandhari, mother of the Kauravas, who holds Krishna responsible for the war. She curses him that he will witness a civil war in the Yadu clan, and he will die in the forest, shot by a hunter who will mistake him for an animal.

56

Both value exchange

In Vedic literature, the act of dharma is embedded in the ritual of yagna. During the yagna, the yajaman feeds the devata in the hope that the devata satisfies his desire. The yajaman gives in order to receive; there is no obligation, no give and take, as in a contract. A good yajaman sees his giving as a repayment of loans from his previous lives—hence there is no demand, no expectation. In an ideal world, we will only give, not seek or take. Such behaviour is possible only when we overcome our desires, like a hermit, and find satisfaction in satisfying other people's desires. That is what Ram and Krishna do. They seek nothing. They only give. They are not hungry yet they perform yagna, their social obligations, to satisfy other people's hunger.

That being said, it is difficult to judge if a person is following dharma or not. For dharma is located in intention, and intention is intangible. Others cannot see it nor measure it. In the *Ramayana*, Ram upholds dharma at all times, and is reviled for it. In the *Mahabharata*, Krishna helps the Pandavas uphold dharma, and discovers how challenging it is.

Helping people sounds very easy but the *Ramayana* and the *Mahabharata* demonstrate that it is not so simple. Who should one feed? Who should one not feed? Whose appetite should be indulged? Who needs to be disciplined? Ram and the Pandavas are often caught in ethical dilemmas or dharma-sankat.

People often translate dharma as righteousness. This assumes some action is always right, but according to karma, even a noble action can have the most unfortunate unforeseen consequences that we become responsible for. For example, keeping a promise is a good thing, right? But when Dasharatha keeps his promise, it means sending Ram to the forest. Should he or shouldn't he? That is dharma-sankat.

In the *Ramayana*, Sugriva asks Ram to shoot Vali while the two are engaged in a duel. By the rules of civilized conduct, this is adharma. Ideally, a warrior should face his opponent. Yet, Ram agrees to this act. Why? Because, here, he is not the leader, he is following the instructions of Sugriva, who is the leader. In doing so, Ram forever is tainted as the one who killed Vali unfairly. If Ram had faced Vali and killed him, he would have become the king of Kishkinda, not Sugriva, for he would then have been the leader, not Sugriva.

In the *Mahabharata*, Arjuna realizes that the war at Kurukshetra involves killing family members. But is it not dharma to provide for and protect family members? Krishna then narrates how humans create the boundary between self and others, and how arbitrarily we protect who we consider self and fight those we consider the other. Arjuna considers the Kauravas family but the Kauravas don't reciprocate this feeling. They refuse to return his kingdom. If he does not fight them and recover his kingdom, he will be going against dharma, for he will be permitting the strong to feed on the weak, thus going against the code of Kshatriyas. So, Arjuna fights the war. It may just be a war, but he has to pay a terrible price. He has to watch his children die as well.

So, both epics draw attention to ethical decisions and dilemmas that kings have to face all the time as they nourish their subjects. They do not have a romantic notion of what is right and what is wrong. Upholding dharma does not guarantee happiness—for that, one has to pursue kama, artha and moksha. Dharma merely guarantees stability for the world at large, by self-regulating human hunger in the best of times, or restraining it by using force in the worst of times.

Conclusion:
Dharma in Progress

In Hindu mythology, unenlightened beings are hungry, frightened and restless. Enlightened beings are neither hungry, nor frightened, nor restless. Brahma and his children—devas, asuras, rakshasas, yakshas, garudas, nagas—are hungry, frightened and restless. Shiva and Vishnu, however, are enlightened beings. So, neither is hungry, frightened or restless.

But Shiva is distant, meditating atop a mountain, and needs to be coaxed by the Goddess to participate in worldly affairs. Vishnu, by contrast, asleep on the ocean of milk, wakes up to the cries of the earth-cow (Bhu-devi) and descends (avatarana) to earth (Bhu-loka) to relieve her of her burden, by establishing dharma.

Dharma cannot be established without empathy—and getting humans to empathize is not easy. The *Ramayana* and *Mahabharata* reveal how Ram and Krishna struggle in this enterprise.

Ram's divinity is passive, so passive that he has to be constantly reminded that he is Vishnu. He simply submits to the demands made on the body he occupies, the body of the eldest son of a royal family. He does what is expected of him. He has no expectations of others. So he never demands obedience; he simply commands it. When he witnesses the people of Ayodhya gossip about his wife, about her character, about her relations with Ravana, his worst fears come true. When he meets Sita for the first time after killing Ravana, he insists on meeting her in public, and publicly informs her that by liberating her he has done his duty as a member of the royal family, and has restored its honour by killing Ravana. He then tells her that she is free to go with any man she wishes to, for he, as a king, cannot accept her as his queen. This is not a god talking. This is a man talking. God is not challenging the ways of man, only witnessing them. The Raghu family's reputation demands that the queen be above gossip. The circumstances have made Sita gossip-fodder. And so, Ram rejects her. But Sita insists on returning to Ayodhya with Ram, and even conducts the fire test (agni-pariksha) to prove she is pure. But that is not the point. Gossip does not care for facts. And impurity is hardly a reason to abandon someone. More than impurity of the body, a king has to be concerned with the purity of reputation. Eventually, reputation prevails, and as king, Ram banishes Sita, whose sojourn in Lanka does irreparable damage to the royal reputation. Sita does not return to Ayodhya. Ram is thus helpless before the demands of kingship. He faces it stoically, and with grace.

Krishna's divinity is active. But he is as helpless as Ram in trying to change human behaviour. He speaks of dharma, but people speak of justice (nyaya) and vengeance (pratishodh). Dharma is based on empathy for the other, while justice and vengeance are based on healing the wounded self. Dharma is about looking beyond one's hunger and fear, at the hunger and fear of others. Krishna wants the Kauravas to care for the Pandavas, but despite all his efforts, they refuse to share with their brothers, using law and force to get their way. So the Pandavas fight—but for what? To get back their land, to get justice, to punish the oppressors— these reasons alone would make the war at Kurukshetra like any other war. Not dharma. In dharma, there are no heroes or villains or victims. The Pandavas have to fight to get back the land that is their livelihood, however, they don't have to hate those who usurped the land. Hatred indulges the ego (aham). They have to do what they have to do as their survival is at stake, not because the Kauravas need to be taught a lesson. No one can teach anyone a lesson; people have to realize it themselves. Krishna watches helpless as despite singing the Bhagavad Gita, Arjuna remains insecure about the war. His motivation is eventually fuelled only when he learns how his teacher orchestrates the killing of his favourite son, Abhimanyu. Bhima and Draupadi are driven by vengeance. They get their revenge but they also lose their children. Bhima loses Ghatotkacha. Draupadi loses her five sons. They are heartbroken, continue to feel sorry for themselves, and stay angry with the Kauravas and their parents. Indeed, despite punishing the Kauravas with death, Yudhishithira cannot handle the presence of his cousins in paradise (swarga). He just cannot forgive. Thus, he clings to his wounded self with such intensity that he is unable to empathize, Krishna's presence notwithstanding. And as for the Kauravas, their blindfolded mother refuses to see her children as villains. For her, they are victims, and so in rage and continuing blindness, she curses Krishna. He accepts it with affection, and hugs the angry, heartbroken mother.

The idea of divinity in Hinduism is very different from other mythologies. It is not an all-powerful deity who punishes those who disobey. Vishnu is not a judge. Ram and Krishna are not role models, as their contexts are different.

Divinity in Hinduism is the human potential to rise above our animal nature. It is that which enables us to live a life without hunger or anxiety. It is that which enables us to empathize with the hunger and anxiety of those around us. It is also that which enables us to recognize that while we can give food, security and knowledge, we cannot make anyone wise. That is a personal journey.

The limitless ones have to patiently watch the struggles and the suffering of the limited ones, who fetter themselves. Like a parent dealing with a stubborn but stupid child, all God can do is love as humans struggle with the animal instincts within and the forest without, so as to live in dharma.

Acknowledgements

- Alf Hiltebeitel, whose works confirmed and clarified many concepts related to dharma and the structure of the epics.

- Kapish for his persistence.

- Ritu who did initial research on the idea of deriving a book from my columns on the two great epics of India.

- Partho who played a key role in framing the book in its current form.

- Harpreet who helped me make the book more reader-friendly.

- Prateek Pattanaik for his help in locating Odia novels based on the epics, and Smitha Baruah who helped me research Assamese novels.

Recommended Reading

- Flood, Gavin. *An Introduction to Hinduism*. New Delhi: Cambridge University Press, 1998.
- Hiltebeitel, Alf. *Dharma: Dimensions in Asian Spirituality*. Honolulu: University of Hawaii Press, 2010.
- ———. *Cult of Draupadi, Vol I*. Chicago: University of Chicago Press, 1988.
- ———. *Rethinking India's Oral and Classical Epics: Draupadi among Rajputs, Muslims, and Dalits*. Chicago: University of Chicago Press, 1999.
- Jaini, Padmanabh S. *The Jaina Path of Purification*. New Delhi: Motilal Banarsidass Publishers, 1979.
- Mani, Vettam. *Puranic Encyclopaedia*. New Delhi: Motilal Banarsidass Publishers, 1996.
- Mazumdar, Subhash. *Who Is Who in the Mahabharata*. Bombay: Bharataiya Vidya Bhavan, 1988.
- Olivelle, Patrick. *Dharma: Studies in its Semantic, Cultural and Religious History*. New Delhi: Motilal Banarsidass Publishers, 2009.
- Sen, Makhan Lal. *The Ramayana of Valmiki*. Delhi: Munshiram Manoharlal, 1978.
- Staal, Frits. *Discovering the Vedas*. New Delhi: Penguin Books India, 2008.
- Subramaniam, Kamala. *Srimad Bhagavatam*. Mumbai: Bharatiya Vidya Bhavan, 1987.
- ———. *Mahabharata*. Mumbai: Bharatiya Vidya Bhavan, 1988.
- ———. *Ramayana*. Mumbai: Bharatiya Vidya Bhavan, 1992.

My Gita

By Devdutt Pattanaik

In *My Gita*, acclaimed mythologist Devdutt Pattanaik demystifies the *Bhagavad Gita* for the contemporary reader. His unique approach—thematic rather than verse by verse makes the ancient treatise eminently accessible, combined as it is with his trademark illustrations and simple diagrams.

In a world that seems spellbound by argument over dialogue, vivaad over samvaad, Devdutt highlights how Krishna nudges Arjuna to understand rather than judge his relationships. This becomes relevant today when we are increasingly indulging and isolating the self (self improvement, self actualization, self realization—even selfies!).We forget that we live in an ecosystem of others, where we can nourish each other with food, love and meaning, even when we fight. So let *My Gita* inform *your* Gita.

'[Devdutt Pattanaik's] subjective and diplomatic craft continues to shine through in his new book. [My Gita] marks his transition from mythology to philosophy—one that he makes with deftness and skill.'

—*Scroll.in*

'While [Devdutt's books are] a quick read, the lessons [they] offer are invaluable and will last a long time.'

—*Business Today*

[Devdutt] is a master storyteller, often with delightful new nuances.

—*India Today*

My Hanuman Chalisa

By Devdutt Pattanaik

A reflection on one of Hinduism's most popular prayers

'Every time I experience negativity in the world, and in myself, every time I encounter jealousy, rage, and frustration manifesting as violation and violence, I hear, or read, the Hanuman Chalisa. Composed over four hundred years ago by Tulsidas, its simple words (in Awadhi, a dialect of Hindi) and its simple metre (dohas and chaupais) musically evoke the mythology, history, and mystery of Hanuman, the much-loved Hindu deity, through whom Vedic wisdom reaches the masses.

As verse follows verse, my frightened, crumpled mind begins to expand with knowledge and insight, and my faith in humanity, both within and without, is restored.'

'I believe Pattanaik has found the pulse of how Hinduism wants to be understood in the 21st century—with his unique intelligence, he is able to speak both to the liberal mind within the fold of the religion as well as the illiberal one that stands as its gatekeeper.'

—Arshia Sattar, *Outlook*

'A treasure trove of mythological information, one marvels at the amount of research that has gone into penning the text... Enlightening, informative, lending itself to multiple debates and a metaphysical treat, this book is infinitely precious.'

—Kankana Basu, *Deccan Chronicle*

'Even those not interested in Hinduism will go through his work to see the spin he puts on a well-loved tradition and perhaps understand why so many generations have thumbed through the original at crucial moments in their lives.'

—Anjana Basu, *author of Rhythms of Darkness*